A Kiss At Midn

Third Edition
Dec 2019

A Kiss At Midnight

A KISS AT MIDNIGHT
NICK ARCHER

A Kiss At Midnight

PROLOGUE
STRIKE TWO

It screams again. The piercing wail filling the moist air, hitting the damp walls, bouncing back. It fills the room, and it is a big room.

The ceiling is thirty feet high, at least. Steel girders, red from rust, wet from the air, stretch from edge to edge, beneath a rising apex; exposed ribs beneath a giant's spine.

Dripping. Rivulets of water run along the corrugated iron ceiling, clinging to it until gravity overwhelms its grip of the metal and the drop tumbles helplessly. Sometimes, they splash onto the spanning girders, others fall the remaining twenty feet to join their fallen comrades forming puddles on the concrete floor below.

Travis concentrates on the puddle by his bare feet, as the screaming reaches an ear-shattering climax. He can barely hear the man's whimpering beneath the shrill voice of the drill, and is thankful for it.

When the drill does stop, and the screaming along with it, Travis tenses himself. The man's crying returns to his ears, worse than before. Even through the gag, his sobs of pain are driven like a spike through Travis's chest.

He doesn't look up. Keeps his eyes down, at the puddle. The water around his toes, the stained concrete under the transparent film, the tiny pebbles set into the floor.

They have been there for years, mixed into the concrete, poured and set, condemned to remain there for more years until the building is destroyed. And then, where will they go?

There is a sharp whistle.

Travis's heart leaps. Ignores it.

Pebbles. Formed over millions of years on beaches, worn smooth over time beyond comprehension, brought here, used. When the floor is removed, the pebbles will continue on. Dumped on a landfill for a time, broken down, repurposed.

Footsteps, coming closer.

Perhaps they'll end up on someone's driveway, or lining a fish tank, or skipped across a pond -

Large hands, rough and strong, grab at Travis's face. He

resists, but the strength in a pair of biceps is greater than that in his neck, and it is wrenched to his left.

The first thing Travis sees is the puddles. They are not pure and clear like the one beneath his feet. Travis cannot see the concrete floor under them. The pebbles there are swamped beneath the redness.

A moan escapes his mouth. Bile rises in his chest but somehow does not.

The man's head is craned backwards, his eyes staring skyward, wide but alive. The dirty gag pulls his mouth back into an awkward smile that contradicts the agony of his face. His mouth is wet, foamy spittle running down his chin. He is sobbing. Deep breaths in that fuel explosive, rhythmic exhalations of unfiltered misery.

The hands hold Travis's head, forcing him to look.

If he had not heard, Travis might not have been able to understand what had happen to the man, such is the mess. The blue denim that once covered the man's right thigh is now a tattered mess, but with barely any blue to be seen amongst the red. The wound itself is unseen, but stringy fibres reach out from it, indistinguishable as the material of his jeans or his flesh.

The man must feel Travis's eyes on him, because his head lolls towards him. A gaze praying for help. Help that Travis could not give if he wanted to.

The truth is, however, that he resents the man. His name is Matt and Travis wishes that he had never met him. That is not to say that he did not feel pity for Matt, and the indescribable pain he must now be in, but it was *Matt's* fault that Travis was sat, bound tightly to a chair, only twelve feet away.

There is water dripping, fatter drops, a faster pour. Travis cannot help but glance over to where two other men are stood by a wall. One is hosing water along the metal bit of the drill, gripped firmly by the other man.

The one holding the drill looks at Travis. He knows his name is Baxter, but does not know the others in the room.

Travis cannot make sense of what the water washes from the large drill bit, the sort of piece used to drill holes large enough for small pipes, but some of it falls to the ground in thick, wet chunks.

This time, Travis does vomit.

His throat expels it into his mouth where it can go no further. The thick, stinging fluid fills the cavity and starts to pour back down the only way it can.

Travis's eyes widen. He coughs into the gag, choking, reflexes making him jerk and buck in the chair, pulling against his restraints.

Baxter looks over at him. He is a tall man, of Congolese

origin, with broad shoulders but a slim waist, wearing a t-shirt with cut off sleeves that show off arms that are both slender and muscular. He frowns and shakes his head in irritation, jerks his head.

'Take the gag off the daft fucker.' His accent is thick, east-London.

The man holding Travis's head, broad-shouldered and bearded, with a deep, badly-healed cut on his upper lip, does so. He rips the dirty material away, more concerned with not getting vomit on his hands rather than Travis's well-being.

Coughing and belching, Travis lurches forward in his chair. The contents of his stomach tumble down his chin onto his chest. His body, having resented the return of its offering, retches again and sends a second helping.

'Fucking hell!' The man with the strong hands steps backwards as yellow-brown liquid gushes onto the ground before Travis.

His puddle is no longer transparent.

Travis cuts an altogether opposing vision to Baxter. Average height and build, a pale, freckled complexion and a mop of ginger hair hangs, lank with sweat across his eyes.

Boot steps echo across the room. Travis peers up to see Baxter walking towards him, the large drill hanging in his hand. He stops, looking down at him. Then points the drill.

'Better?'

Travis gulps, mouth open, his voice lost. He stares at the drill.

'Good.' Baxter replies to the non-answer and walks towards Matt again. 'I wouldn't want to you miss it this time. And remember, Travis, your mate, Matt, here; he's on strike two.'

Travis's eyes widen. Matt's see Baxter advance towards him, starts to shout through his gag, shakes his head, eyes so wide they might roll out of their sockets.

Travis turns his head, but inevitably, the strong hands grab his jaw and force his head to look. There is no foreplay, no lead up or verbal preface. The second and third man grab Matt, one about his shoulders, the other his right leg. Baxter turns the drill vertically, rests the wide, jagged drill bit against the top of Matt's other thigh and squeezes the trigger.

Screaming again.

This time Travis can hear Matt's wailing through the gag and knows that they will be soon be his own.

A Kiss At Midnight

A Kiss At Midnight

A Kiss At Midnight

So runs my dream, but what am I?
An infant crying in the night
An infant crying for the light
And with no language but a cry.

- 'In Memoriam A.H.H.', Lord Alfred Tennyson, 1849

A Kiss At Midnight

1

The girl sits on the bed, her face impassive, and her body inexpressive. Waiting. Like the flashing icon on a word document, lifeless without instruction.

This is how Michael likes them.

He swirls the brandy in his balloon, listening to the ice clink as it noisily circumnavigates the glass. A clock ticks somewhere in the adjoining room, voices can be heard outside on the street. A window is open somewhere. He should have shut that. Even seven floors up, the noise of Saturday binge-drinkers is as clear as if they were in the next room.

Damnit, I should have shut that God-damned window.

He berates himself silently, making sure to keep the

emotion from his face.

The suite is a large one, though not the biggest or most lavish in the hotel. Third perhaps. Not that this girl would know. To her, this suite is something she'd find at the top of a Dubai skyscraper. Michael knows better. He's been to Dubai. He's stayed in those hotels, and you wouldn't find girls like *this* in *those* hotels.

Michael inhales slowly, takes a long sip of the brandy, keeping his eyes on the girl. His eyes flick to his glass, then back.

He lets the liquid slide to the back of his throat, holds it there for a moment, then swallows.

There it is. The girl licks her lips involuntarily. She probably doesn't even know that she's done it.

Nearly there.

A siren. Loud and piercing. An ambulance chasing through the city, probably to breathe life back into some twenty-year old idiot who has yet to learn how much is too much.

He waits until its wailing passes away, then slowly lets the glass drop to the arm of the chair he is sat in. Straightens his tie against his shirt, neatens the tiepin. Takes his time doing it. Then uses a finger to push a few stray hairs back into place, tucking them in amongst the rest of his blonde hair. At 56, he is proud to still have a good head of hair, thick too. He had noticed it starting to thin at the top, but in such a place that he could continue to sweep his fringe backwards to conceal it.

A creak.

His eyes shoot up, locking on the girl. She freezes, but it is clear she has moved. One of her legs has shifted, presumably to stave off the onset of pins and needles.

He had her sit on the bed, her legs tucked under her around thirty-five minutes ago. She hadn't moved since.

It was time.

Michael lets a smile creep across his face. An instruction. The girl comes out of default mode and smiles back obediently.

A rattle. His phone rings silently on the table beside him.

This time he cannot help but let out a frustrated sigh and looks over. The screen flashes up the name Ian.

Tapping his fingernails on the brandy balloon, he looks at the girl, his eyes narrowed in anger. She looks back at him, then drops her eyes.

The rattling of plastic against glass continues for several long seconds, before stopping.

Silence, then, or as close to it as possible considering the open window and over-loud revellers below.

Michael takes a sip, quick this time, brings himself back

to the present, speaks, 'Stand up.'

The girl does as asked. She swings her legs over the edge of the bed and lifts herself into stands. She is unsteady, one foot having gone to sleep. Michael sees the discomfort in her face as she gingerly touches a high-heeled foot to the carpet.

She is wearing a sequinned gold dress. Tacky and short. It clings to her figure, but she has none to speak of.

Irrelevant.

'Kneel,' Michael commands, and she does, but there is a flicker of something now.

The girl is now on her knees, how she was on the bed. The pins and needle obviously still bother her. Her feet twitch under her.

'Crawl to me.'

Another instruction carried out. The girl drops forward to her hands and begins to move forward, slowly. This she knows; this is not new to her. She drops the small of her back, locks eyes with him. Every step with her arms and legs is exaggerated, designed to entice.

'Stop.' Michael makes sure that she hears the exasperation in his voice. He stares at her for a moment, as if challenging her to come up with a reason as to why he has stopped her advance.

She frowns a little, thinking, convinced she has done

nothing wrong. This is what he wanted. This is what she always does.

Michael rolls his eyes, 'Don't use your hands. On your knees only.'

A flash of annoyance in her eyes.

Yes.

There it is.

Michael grips the glass. Without a word, the girl rises back to her knees and starts to shuffle forward. It is awkward and ungainly, a jerky motion that lands her uncomfortably before him, between his knees.

He looks down at her, smiling. He knows that she knows this smile. She knows what is next.

'Well then?'

She smiles a practised smile, but behind it there is loathing. She's given a lot of blow-jobs that she'd rather she hadn't, but this one is pushing her. And Michael knows it.

The girl reaches up and puts her hand on his crotch.

Michael speaks sharply, 'What on earth are you doing?'

The girl's eyes widen. Her mouths forms an 'I' but she has never had to explain her actions. They are greatly self-explanatory. Especially to someone who has led her to this point and not only seems surprised, but disgusted at her activity.

Michael is shaking her head at her, slowly and derisively. He takes in an exaggerated breath, exhales heavily. Says nothing. The girl looks around. She is done. Out of her comfort zone. A situation out of her control.

'Open your mouth.'

The words stun her. She doesn't.

Michael gives her a sideways look, and then leans over to his jacket on the chair. He reaches into the inside pocket and removes a wad of cash.

Placing it on the glass table beside them, he fans it out. He has already paid her, so this is extra. Double what he has given her an hour ago.

Her eyes settle on it, remain on it as she opens her mouth.

Michael grins and leans forward, then uses a finger to lift her chin, directing her mouth towards him. The girl keeps her eyes on the money as Michael dips his finger into the brandy.

He then moves into the gaping maw and runs it along her tongue. Her lips starts to move towards each other, but Michael states firmly, 'No. Open.'

She obeys. Eyes still on the money.

Michael runs his finger along her tongue, depositing the brandy, then moves to the row of molars on her left. He presses down, pulls his finger along them, making them squeak.

The girl's throat pulses. Her eyes glisten.

A rattle. Plastic on glass again.

Michael looks over at his phone. *Ian.* It's fine this time. He's done.

He removes his finger and wipes any moisture on her gold dress. She doesn't move. Doesn't close.

'You can go now,' he says sharply, then in one movement swipes the pile of cash onto the floor as he snatches up his phone.

He steps over the girl, still on her knees, as she pick the notes up. Her movements are frantic; she wants to leave quickly.

Michael, crossing to that open window, presses answer, 'Ian, yes, sorry, I missed your call. You're in the lobby? Great, I'll meet you in the bar.'

He listens to the reply, downs the remains of his drink. The ice is now long melted.

'Please, thanks; I'll take a brandy.'

*

It is A Bar Called Cafe.

At quarter past eight on this, like most Saturday nights of the year, it is heaving. Patrons stacked shoulder to

A Kiss At Midnight

shoulder at the bar, three or four rows deep. Each is next to be served, each one here before the person beside them, living outside of a shared chronology.

Time started when they arrived. There was no before.

A dozen eyes stare unblinking across the counter top, trying to catch the eye of the three bar persons bustling up and down the narrow space between the pumps and the spirits stacked on shelves at the back. A young man with a deathly complexion, shaved scalp and dark beard to his solar plexus, and earlobes so long you could stick your finger through them; he steps back and forth with practised skill, three bottles of Peroni in one hand, flicking caps off with an opener in the other. He places them on the bar, mouths something to the skinny male student thrusting money at him, takes it, charges for four bottles at the till, hands back the change and moves on.

Beside him two young women, move around him in a practised dance. The first has caramel skin that betrays her dual heritage, a mother from Portugal, a father's parents from Uganda; a blend that, along with her green eyes, tattooed collar bone, and sleeved-shoulders makes her the second choice of server to most of the men on bar, given the choice. The other girl is from Sweden, and is the female archetype of the country. Tall, fair-skinned and fair-haired. She sports the most conventional look of the three, and the least body art; a small rose on the underside of her wrist.

The Swede slips gracefully between her colleagues, smiling genuinely at her customers as she serves them swiftly, politely discouraging prolonged conversation whilst still ensuring a succession of tips. An older man catches her next, orders a pint of Carling that she immediately starts at the pump right beside her. He leans over and starts talking to her, smiling with what he clearly hopes is charm. Although she cannot hear him over the pounding bass of the music, she nods without commitment to whatever it is he might be saying.

The lager reaches its limit near the top of the glass and she releases the handles, pushes it back a fraction to encourage a squirt of foam into the top. Handing it back, he takes it from her before she can place it on the bar mat, touching her hand. She manages to snatch her hand away before he can grab it. He means no real harm, she can tell, but she mouths the cost of the drink before he can say anything. He hands her a five pound note and tells her to keep the change. She smiles gratefully and turns to the till.

A moment's respite at the open cash drawer, before slamming it shut and turning again to the bar. A woman this time, well-dressed with flawless make-up and a narrow face. The Swede nods at her, but cannot make out what she is saying. Leans in further. The woman's voice, higher than most of the males here, makes her just understandable.

'I'm looking for Camilla!'

*

'I really love your eyes, innit?'

It is not clear if it is a question or a statement.

'They're proper green.'

Definitely a statement, though its purpose is unclear.

Camilla snaps off the caps of the two bottles of Peroni, places them on the bar before the young man in the over-sized baseball cap, who talks in a pitch several bars lower than is natural. He is the kind of person that makes her glad there is a bar between them. She feels sorry for the numerous girls tonight that will not have the luxury of such a barrier.

'Anything else?' Camilla mouths back at him. He grins, nodding in reverse. The movement starting low, his chin jerking up, 'Yeah, your number, innit?'

Camilla smiles. She has several methods of rejecting such plays, each one suited to the type of person she is

A Kiss At Midnight

facing; here she opts for number 3. 'Sorry, my boyfriend wouldn't approve. He's the one of the door.'

Baseball cap glances over, looking at both of the two gym-built hulks with the blue badges on their arms, stood like sentinels at the entrance. He glances back at Camilla, proffers a twenty pound note, 'Alright, safe.' He doesn't wait for his change.

Camilla turns to the back bar, taps the items into the till's screen. As the drawer bounces open, someone grabs her arm.

She looks over, then up at the tall blonde, holding onto her wrist. 'I was trying to call you.'

Camilla shrugs, tucks in the cash, takes the change, pockets it, 'Couldn't hear you, Linnea. What's up?'

'Someone's here to see you.'

'Who?'

Linnea turns and points her slender, pale finger towards the end of the bar. Camilla follows it and sees the well-dressed woman stood, staring intently back at her. The woman smiles nervously, and gives a little wave.

Camilla's heart leaps. She gives a little wave back, 'Tell Tony I'm taking my break.'

'What? We're slammed.'

'Tell him to take it up with Sam,' Camilla shoots back challengingly and although Linnea gives her a sharp look in return, she says nothing.

As Linnea catches the eye of another jostling patron and returns to the battle at the front, Camilla walks down to the end of the bar and slips through the gap. A rotund boy of sixteen is busy stacking glasses into the washer, and he moves aside quickly as she passes, pushing her way into the crowds.

There is more space beyond the bar area. A lot of people shoving themselves against the bar, but those who are not are spread out more evenly, stood against tall tables dotted around, or sat in the large window at the front on wooden benches. The bar has an unfinished feel, as is the current fashion, but Sam has not gone with the contrived, 'rip out half a wall to make it look bad,' he simply left it bare. Pipes, girders, support beams. He decided that if he did not have to pay to 'finish' it, then why should he? He'd ride this trend until it ran out, then fork out for plaster and paint.

Camilla threads her way towards the end of bar, and finds the woman making her way to her, but before they can connect, a hand, uninvited, snakes around her waist and tries to pull her. She leans away and turns her head to see a dimpled face that is too small for the beard it hides behind. Hot breath, acidic with stale liquor washes across her and she cannot help but lean away as it speaks,

'You've been working hard. Have a drink with me.'

Camilla gives a perfunctory smile and replies, 'And I'm still working. Let go.'

With disappointing predictability, the refusal only urges the Small Face on. As she turns away, his arms moves around her stomach, stopping her escape, 'Come on. Just do a shot with us.'

Anger ignites in the pit of her belly. It's an Option 5 scenario. Camilla turns to him and his two friends, grinning manically at the pantomime, and smiles at them.

Without warning, her hand shoots out to his crotch and grabs a firm handful of what little there is. For a second, Small Face's grin widens, but then her grip tightens. He lets out a whimper and leans in, allowing her to press her forehead against his, look into his eyes and say, 'Unless you want to take these home in a little bag, you'll take your hands off me.'

The hand slithers away and she releases him. From the doorway, one of the bouncers is looking over with interest, but Camilla gives him a wink to indicate that all is fine. He nods back.

Camilla turns away, back to the bar and the woman stood watching with wide-eyed interest. Returning her focus to the woman, she moves through the last remaining patrons.

They find themselves together, away from the throng, and straight away, the woman offers her hand to Camilla. She speaks, but her words are lost in the noise, so she leans in. Her perfume is overwhelming, clearly expensive, Camilla can say, and her hand is soft, her grip firm.

'Hi, Camilla,' the woman says again, speaking directly into her ear. 'It's so nice to finally meet you. I'm Cassandra.'

Camilla nods, and replies, 'I know. It's nice to meet you too.'

Cassandra smiles, waiting for Camilla to say or do more, but Camilla's head is spinning. The noise of the bar, Cassandra's scent, the promise of this meeting.

The older woman clearly sees her having trouble and leans in again, 'Should we go somewhere to talk?'

Camilla's heart pounds. She nods and still holding Cassandra's hand, pulls her through the crowd to the door at the end that leads to her flat.

2

Michael exits the lift into the hotel's lobby. He is now wearing his jacket over his shirt and a long overcoat draped over his arm. He walks without urgency through the several people queuing restlessly at the reception desk, some in couples, most on their own, all with baggage laid at their feet. The sign for the Castle View hotel is emblazoned over the head of the slim man with a feminine disposition working the desk.

Michael had used this hotel for many years, since before its name change from the Rutland Square Hotel, throughout its several refurbishments, the most recent meaning the gutting of the sixth floor and inclusion of three new suites, in addition to a revamped penthouse and conference centre. A successful local entrepreneur and businessman, he had been, in previous years, top of the list of people asked to talk at numerous events and dinners.

Leaving the lobby behind, Michael climbs the steps to the bar and restaurant area and quickly spots Ian sat on a stool at the bar. An unremarkable man, Ian would have been overlooked by anyone not looking specifically for him. A round face, short dark hair, clean-shaven, he was portly, not obese, nor overly tall, nor by any means short. He was the very definition of average. What set him apart was his incredible aptitude for numeracy and the diegetic memory that supported it.

Ian is swallowing a vodka as he sees Michael walking in, trying to say hello at the same time, the resulting movement being a lot of waving his hands; part greeting, part apology, part offer of a drink.

Michael nods, 'Yes, the same, Ian. I'll be over here.'

Ian nods and raises a finger to the barman as Michael weaves through the busy bar to one of the pairs of sofas laid out on the perimeter of the bar, finding a vacant seat. A flat screen television is set into the wall beside them, the image a silent flickering fireplace intended to create ambience. There are several of these booths, each with its own faux fireplace set into walls with wallpaper printed with books. It's designed to be charming, but Michael finds it an irritation. It's a good idea. Effective, but not expensive. He wishes he'd had it.

Ian arrives, with a briefcase hanging from his fingers and a pair of glasses filled with clear liquid, handing one to Michael before sitting on the opposing sofa with the plopping sound of cushions losing air suddenly. He speaks rapidly as he fidgets, finding a comfortable position on the low-backed seat, 'Sorry I kept ringing; I was worried that they'd call early.'

Michael grins, 'I was watching the time, Ian. Don't worry.'

Ian grimaces, 'I'm paid to worry. It's literally half my job.' As he speaks, he proceeds to open the briefcase from its place by his feet and take out a small sheaf of papers, stapled together in the top corner, dropping it onto the coffee table between them, 'And I worry about you the most, Michael.'

'Well, bless you, Ian.'

'Michael, we've worked together a long time, but at the end of the day, if you don't make money, neither do I.'

Michael rolls his eyes, tosses back half the vodka, 'Didn't we have this conversation this morning?'

'And chances are we'll be having it again at breakfast, especially if this doesn't pan out,' Ian replies bluntly, tapping a finger on the file. The top sheet shows a selection of photographs portraying a crop of buildings, most long and low with a large two-storey in the rear. That large building is shown in greater detail in the remaining few images. At the top are the words, printed in a large, blocky font.

£450,000.

Michael glances down at it and shrugs. Ian shudders at the sight, 'Your outward appearance of calm concerns me.'

'And as you stated; so it should,' Michael replies coolly, 'But it's not an 'appearance'. I am calm. Confident.'

Ian bites his inner lip, takes a sip of the vodka, checks his phone. No call. He looks over at Michael, who is staring blindly into the flames. The flames, having long since burnt out their fuel and reduced to ashes, flicker mockingly from beyond the grave; like canned laughter, recorded most of a century ago, voices of the dead echoing into the present.

Ian ventures a question, convinced that he doesn't want to know the answer, 'Tell me about the other property. Is it a go?'

Michael half nods, 'So far as I know.'

Ian shakes his head, leans forward suddenly, jerking his glass at Michael, 'Christ, will you take this seriously.' He notices Michael's jovial smile fade and lowers his voice respectfully, 'Please. I'm trying to keep you afloat, Michael. You have to keep me informed.'

'There is currently nothing more to inform you of, Ian,' Michael says, keeping eye contact to assure him of the honesty of his reply, rather than as a reproach, 'The seller is very keen.'

Ian blinks, thinking, 'How much is he asking?'

Michael smiles, 'Two-fifty.'

'For the whole lot?'

'The building, the business. The works.'

'Aside from the property value, the business itself is viable?'

Michael nods, 'Very.'

'Will he stay on to run it?'

Michael shakes his head, screwing up his mouth, 'No. He's making a run for it. Moving abroad as soon as the sale goes through.'

Ian sits back slowly, thinking, running numbers through his head, 'Yeah, okay. We could do this. This could work, Michael.'

'I know.'

'Seriously. Sink some funds into this venture you've found, keep things just ticking over. We'll buy some cheap land out in Spain or France, hold it there, just in case. You might just make it through, Michael. I mean, *these* buyers are a stroke of luck. I'm not asking questions but if they're able to move that sort of money around so quickly...'

'You've been watching too much Ozark, Ian.'

'Fine. You don't want to know, then I don't want to know. Saves me a lot of paperwork anyway. Let's not piss them off though, just in case.'

Michael rolls his eyes, 'In case what?'

Suddenly, a shrill noise cuts through the monologue, the standard Nokia theme. Two pairs of eyes go to it, Ian's hand snatches it up, 'In case of – whatever. Michael, we *need* this – Hello?'

Ian smiles into the phone affably, as though they can hear his smile, while Michael sits back, nursing the vodka and listening. Ian exchanges niceties with the caller.

'Yes, very well, thank you, and you? Good, great. We are. Are they with you now? Great. Please, go ahead.'

Ian listens, nodding, thinking, his eyes moving left to right rapidly. Michael watches him. He knows what is being said without having to hear it. He waits patiently until Ian exhales, looking deflated.

'I see. Okay, well, if you'll hold, I'll pass the offer on to Michael,' Ian says, then presses mute on the phone before running a hand across his receding hairline, looking like he's just been told he has an incurable disease. He says nothing.

Michael breaks the silence, 'How low?'

Ian doesn't look up, 'They're offering three-twenty five.'

Michael knew it. They had the surveyor look at the property and inevitably found the dry rot in the house's basement, the weakened foundations in the stables and the electrical problems for the site. They only reason they hadn't gone lower was because they hadn't yet discovered the drainage issues in the east field, but that was fine. They wouldn't find that for months, not until long after the deeds were handed over and he was no longer liable for it; he and Ian would work something subtle into the sales contracts to see to that.

Again, he waits, waits for Ian to speak, who keeps looking at the phone as if he's tempted to ask as if he'd misheard. Finally, Ian does make eye contact, and says as confidently as he can, 'It's taking a hit, but we can make it work. So long as the other venture goes well. And we'd need to invest the remaining capital *carefully*. You'd be living on a shoe string, at least for 18 months. Would your wife be okay with that?'

Michael grunts at the mention of her, replies sharply, 'She's not your concern, Ian. She'll be fine.'

Ian holds up an apologetic hand, 'Should I tell them we accept?'

Michael downs his vodka, pauses for a moment, then in one movement places his glass down and holds out his hand for the phone. Ian frowns, then slowly passes it over.

Tapping the button to un-mute the call, Michael puts it to his ear, 'Hi, Michael Clavell here. That offer is a fucking joke. Tell your clients to stick it up their arse.'

*

As soon as Camilla opens the door to the flat, she can smell the smoke.

She pauses, annoyed at it. Cassandra is stood behind her, still on the stairs, as there is only a narrow landing before the door. The door at the bottom that leads back into the bar cuts off about half of the loud music, leaving a thudding murmur in the quieter staircase.

Cassandra looks up at Camilla, offers a smile that asks if everything is all right. To this, Camilla can only return the gesture and pretend she has not noticed the smell as she holds the door open, allowing her guest to pass her.

The spring loaded closer pulls the heavy door shut. It clicks on the Yale lock. All that is left of the music below is a distant pounding. It is a well-built building with thick walls and floors, perfect for a living space above something as noisy as an inner city bar. Surprising, considering it used to be nothing more luxurious than a storeroom for the trendy clothes shop that used be where the bar now reigns.

Its previous use means that the greater part of the space is open, in which a small living area, jutting kitchenette, and breakfast table are placed. Stud walls section off a pair of small bedrooms and a tiny bathroom.

The door now closed, Camilla extends an arm, encouraging Cassandra to enter the flat. She watches her look around, taking in the details of the décor. Although Cassandra is obviously a woman of taste, Camilla is pleased in her choices of furniture and the like, and does not feel embarrassed to show off her accommodation.

There is only item that she wishes were not present.

'Sam,' Camilla calls out and the large man sprawled on the white leather, low-backed corner sofa looks at them in surprise.

He quickly swings his legs off the sofa, dusting crumbs from his lap, 'I didn't hear you come in, darling.' Storage Hunters plays loudly on the television, and he quickly pauses it. The room is suddenly uncomfortably silent.

Camilla nods to Cassandra, 'This is my... friend, that I

told you was coming to see me.'

Sam stands abruptly, yet more crumbs falling to the floor as he does. He thrust out his big hand, takes her slender one, shakes it, 'Yeah, nice to meet you. Kimberley, was it?'

'Cassandra,' Cassandra corrects him, politely. It is the first time Camilla has heard her voice properly. It is low, but not unpleasantly so. Articulate and smooth, it has a richness to it, a sing-song quality.

Sam lets her hand go and Camilla puts her hand on Cassandra's elbow, steering her towards the sofa, 'Please, sit down. Do you want a drink?'

God, she sounds so coarse next to Cassandra. Her flat Midlands accent appals her in a way it never had before.

'Just water, thank you.'

Camilla steps away into the kitchen. Sam follows her and she whispers, 'I have a sense of smell, Sam.'

Sam shrugs, 'Relax, I blew the smoke out of the window.'

'Cigars still smell. I could smell it the second I walked in and so can my friend,' she retorts firmly as she takes a glass, and fills it with bottled water from the fridge. She expects no apology, gets none, and adds, more gently, 'Everything else all right up here?'

Sam leans on the counter, 'Fine. Never a problem for

me, darling.'

'Good.' Camilla crosses to where Cassandra has positioned herself on the sofa, on a spot away from Sam's deposited crumbs, and hands her the glass.

'Thank you,' she says, then her eyes fall on Sam, along with Camilla's.

The hint is not lost on Sam, who nonetheless moves in his own time and not before. He grunts and pushes himself away from the worktop, taking his large self towards the door slowly enough to make the point. He grips the door handle, 'I'll leave you ladies to it. Nice to meet you, Cassandra. Camilla, I've made one up and left it in the fridge, but I will need you back downstairs by ten at the latest. Brandon is going early.'

Camilla replies, 'Sure, no problem. I'll bring the mike down with me.'

Sam nods curtly and leaves. For a second, music rushes into the flat and is cut off by the closing door. Camilla, willing him to leave, suddenly wishes he'd come back. Sam is a known quantity; not only is he very much you get what you see, but she knows him very well. Under his coarse and abrupt manner, he is a very kind and considerate man. A good friend.

No, was.

She pushes that thought from her mind and thinks

about Cassandra. This older woman, in her late forties, sophisticated, articulate, clearly wealthy, is far from her comfort zone. Fuck it, that desperation to cling to comfort, to what is known, is what had gotten her into this position. Stuck. Mired in a life she does not want.

'Sit down, please,' Cassandra says suddenly, 'You're making me nervous.' She follows it with a smile that she might have paid money for.

Camilla does as bidden, sitting on the perpendicular edge, amongst the crumbs. She folds her arm across her stomach, an automatic thing, self-conscious about the prominence of her stomach over her belt. Her vest-top, emblazoned with the script AC/DC, divided by a lightning sign, fits her well enough when stood, but she always feels like she spills everywhere when sat. To boot, she was a five foot five inch size ten, a measurement that fits her generous hips but hangs off her small waist awkwardly without the aid of surreptitious clipping or tying.

She feels like a troll sat across from Cassandra. The woman has five inches on her height, at least one dress size down, with everything where it should be, in the proportion that it should be.

'Relax.' That low, smooth voice again. A hand reaching across, taking hers, squeezing it.

Camilla swallows, clears her throat, 'This is... new territory for me.'

'Me too,' Cassandra replies, 'This is not something you do every day.' She laughs. It is like velvet. She wants to say more. A question sits in her eyes, but is restricted by etiquette.

Camilla can see that if she wants this, she must initiate it.

A deep breath.

'Do you want to see him?'

3

Cassandra maintains the smile on her face until Camilla has left the room, having disappeared into one of the bedroom at the rear of the flat. When she is out of sight Cassandra sighs, letting out the tension and disappointment that has built up in her over the last twenty minutes.

He said she was pretty.

All Cassandra can see is a dumpy little barmaid with a bad tattoo of a moth and flowers scrawled across the top of her cleavage. Her green eyes are quite striking, that much she will admit, but to say she is disappointed is as much of an understatement as Michael's verbal review had been an overstatement.

Cassandra looks around the room. It is like the small-space display at Ikea. United, each item of furniture and decoration seems fine. Not great, but reasonable. If you put them on their own they would be brutally ousted as the overpriced, under-designed farce of home living Cassandra knew they were. Then there was the stink of cigars that had hit her as soon as the door had been opened, making her retch internally, though she was able to conceal her disgust.

What bothers her most of all, however, is the Christmas tree propped up on the corner, behind a small armchair. It is, at least, stripped of baubles and lights, and clearly real. 'Its branches and needles are starting to brown and are drooping under their own weight. Once the stench of cigar leaves the room, Cassandra expects the aroma of rotting pine will fill it instead.

She is irked, but reminds herself of why she is here. It helps.

Suffering a little while in this dump would be more than worth it overall.

Talking, low and soothing comes from the back, and a moment later, footsteps on the wooden floor. Cassandra feels her pulse quicken and her mouth suddenly goes dry, all the moisture presumably having gone directly to her palms that she wipes subtly on her long, cream coat.

Camilla reappears, and in her arms is a small baby,

swaddled in a yellow blanket. Cassandra's chest tightens as they sit by her and the scent of talcum powder and formula milk wafts up her nose. She has to stop herself from crying out and snatching the baby from Camilla's arms.

She waits, her hands folded as Camilla settles beside her, holding a dummy so that it stays in the baby's mouth.

Cassandra moves the edge of the blanket so that she can see the baby's face better. There is a flicker of disappointment when the child's eyes are revealed as brown rather than the electric green of his mother's, but it passes quickly. It has a round face and almost no hair, but a small nose and a hint of dimples.

Control over her manner has been lost, and Cassandra knows that she is grinning wildly. Camilla can see it. Is taking pleasure from it. Cassandra resents this loss of control, this momentary handing over of dominance over the situation, but the burning joy in her chest that threatens to burst forth and ignite eclipses it.

'Would you like to hold him?' It is a question that barely needs to be asked, and Cassandra, with as much decorum as she can muster, holds out her arms. Camilla gently moves the baby across and places him into the other woman's embrace.

He fits.

Cassandra's first thought overwhelms her. She gazes down at him, unable to control the smile on her face as he stares back up at her.

'I really don't know how to start this conversation,' Camilla says, sliding away from Cassandra on the sofa, 'I've run it through my head so many times, but I can't –'

Cassandra doesn't look up, but speaks clearly, confidently, 'A hundred thousand was what my husband said. Does that still stand?'

Camilla doesn't answer at first, struggling to find a reply. Perhaps she is deciding if she can get more. Cassandra waits. She can wait all night. The pure joy of feeling the weight in her arms is almost too much to bear.

Camilla finally says, 'Yeah. That's what he said to me. That's... um... that's fair.'

Fair.

Cassandra scoffs inwardly. *What does she know about fair?* Outwardly, she smiles, uses a manicured nail to stroke the baby's cheek. He turns his head. It tickles.

'He's how old?' she asks.

'Eight weeks.'

'How much was he when he was born?'

The question seems to baffle Camilla. Cassandra looks up to see her puzzled expression, 'His weight?'

'Oh,' Camilla cries out, 'Sorry, um. I don't know. I'd have to check his book.'

Cassandra nods and turns the baby around on her knee, so that his head is nestled in her palms, looking up at her. 'Any complications during the birth?'

Camilla shakes her head firmly, 'No. None.'

'Did you have an epidural?'

A firm nod. 'Of course. Fucking hurt.'

Cassandra repositions him so that he is held in place by one hand, using the other to smooth the blanket down from around his face so that she can study his face.

Good God, it is beautiful.

His skin is so smooth and clear. She checks his head; no sign of cradle cap, and she has already counted all his fingers and toes.

Perfect.

Cassandra can feel Camilla's eyes on her. Not defensive, or protective. Nothing like that. Impatient. 'Last question; do you know who the father is?'

Camilla frowns, 'Of course.'

'Alright. Does he know about this?'

Camilla shakes her head, 'He doesn't know... at all.'

'That he has a son?'

Another shake.

'Where is he?'

A Kiss At Midnight

The young woman looks uncomfortable. She fidgets in her seat, eyes scanning the room. 'He's not around. Just... I don't know where. But not here. Not for a while.'

Suddenly a mobile phone rings. They both look over to the coffee table where one is vibrating towards the edge. Camilla grabs it, sees who is calling and answers gruffly, 'Yes, Sam?'

Cassandra turns her attention back to the baby in her lap as Camilla has a conversation that, at least on her side, is very monosyllabic.

She hangs up and says, 'I'm so sorry, they need me downstairs, and I have to settle him again.'

Cassandra smiles, 'Of course.' She stands to hand the baby back over casually, but it kills her to have to do it. Once he is passed back over, she asks, 'Does he have a name?'

For the first time, Camilla looks embarrassed. She half shrugs, half shakes her head, 'No. I – I haven't given him one. It's -'

Cassandra reaches out and touches her arm, 'It's okay, Camilla. He's not registered?'

'No.'

'That's good. Really.'

Camilla appears reassured that she has done the right thing, and Cassandra is content with those final answers.

No name is perfect. She'd only have to change it from whatever chavvy moniker he had been given, and at least the idiot girl had had the good sense not to get him registered. That made things much easier.

Cassandra gives Camilla her dressiest smile, 'Thank you so much for meeting me, Camilla. Honestly, it means everything that you would consider me for this. It must be so hard to be in a position to even think about doing something like this - '

'Do you want him?' The question is blurted out so rapidly, it is more a long word than a sentence.

Cassandra lets a moment pass. Enjoys the panic in Camilla's face, forged by the apparent lack of decision from the buyer. A cold fear of losing the sale.

The baby stirs. Silently content until now, he starts to cry.

*

Michael approaches his car at a trot. There is a spring in his step. He feels alive. Like a skydiver plunging through the air; twenty thousand feet becomes ten thousand in a matter of seconds, the parachute on his back promises his safe delivery to the ground, but there is always that chance it won't open. The jumper knows what he is doing. He's done it a hundred times before, but it only needs that one failure to make it his last jump. That's half the thrill. It's the same for Michael. He's jumped. He's watching the ground racing up to meet him. When the time is right, he'll pull the cord. He just needs to wait.

He walks around from the front of the hotel to the left of the lobby, around a barrier to the small area at the side. A multi-storey car park rises above him, like a concrete giant, crouched over him, watching him trot to his black Mercedes c250 parked at the far end. Clicking the button on his keys, he thinks of Ian in amusement.

He had left him in stunned silence, downing the remainder of his vodka and ordering another.

'What the fuck are you doing?', Ian had uttered, his piggy eyes as wide as they could be, 'Michael, seriously... what did you just do? If you think we can a better offer, fine - '

'We *can* get a better offer,' Michael had interrupted, spinning the phone in his hand.

'But even so... you didn't have to tell them *that*!'

Michael had raised an eyebrow and sat back, 'They'll call back.'

'After that? I don't think they will.'

'They will.'

Ian had thrown his hands up in exasperation, almost throwing himself back into his seat like a toddler having a tantrum. At that, Michael, wished him good night and left without another word.

Now, he slides into the leather seat and turns the engine on. It whispers into life.

The property is in disrepair, but its potential value far exceeds the price tag he and Ian had set out. They hadn't overpriced it, but had worked out what was just under laughable, then added a little more on. The offers were always going to be lower. What Michael knew was that if they did develop the property, either renovating the farmhouse and its outlying stables back into a country home, or converting it into holiday lets, or even bulldozing the whole damn lot and selling the land to other developers, they'd make a profit. When he had bought it, he'd planned on the latter. It would yield the greatest profit, but other things had got in the way. He no longer had the means to follow through with his designs. The rug had been pulled out from under him the previous year and he had been trying to keep from falling over ever since.

He pushes these thoughts from his mind. They make him angry. Frustration swells up quickly and threatens to envelop him. Things beyond his control drive him crazy. Unforeseeable and unavoidable events that affect him make his blood boil.

God grant me the serenity to accept the things I cannot change, the courage to change the things I can, and the wisdom to know the difference.

Michael loathes that saying. His mother said it a lot. It was her excuse to throw her hands up at everything and say 'Oh well, never mind. It wasn't meant to be.' She not only accepted her own limitations but also created them for herself.

The idea of limitation was something Michael had always rejected.

He drops the car into drive and it rolls silently forward. One hand on the wheel, he guides it to the barrier.

There is a chirping noise from within the car, and a pleasant female voice speaks to him.

'You have a message from Ball and Chain. Would you like to hear it?'

He wondered when he'd hear from her this evening. Sighing, he replies to the car, 'Yes.'

A pause.

'The message is; "I'm on my way home. I'll meet you there. We have to talk."'

Michael makes a face of disgust.

'Would you like to reply?'

Bunching his lips in thought, Michael says, 'No.'

An affirmative beep and silence. Michael drums his fingers in thought, running a future conversation in his head as he approaches the barrier where the hidden camera detects his registration number in order to lift it.

It doesn't.

Michael frowns and creeps the car forward. It doesn't even quiver. He backs it up a few feet, tries again, more slowly, but still the barrier does not move.

'Fucking hell!'

He sits there looking around, hoping for a member of the hotel staff to appear but no one does.

Grumbling, he gets out of the car. It's starting to drizzle. Fine rain leaving its mark on the polished black finish of the Mercedes. Leaving it where it is, he heads around the barrier and back into the lobby.

The queue there has gone down, but there is still an elderly foreign couple stood waiting as the effeminate young man hands over their key cards.

Michael taps his foot as he waits. Glances up through the glass doors to the bar, where he can see the back of Ian's bald head where he left him.

'Can I help?' The voice of the receptionist is high.

Michael steps forward, 'The barrier is broken. I can't get my car out.'

The receptionist frowns and smiles at the same time. A bizarre combination. 'It is?' he replies with an upward inflection, and leans over to another area of the desk to look, presumably, at a CCTV monitor. 'Ah, there you are.'

He then goes to another computer and taps a few keys. Michael exhales loudly and leans over the counter, looking at the man intently as he goes about his work, unperturbed.

'Ah, I see. I'm afraid the barrier isn't the issue. The credit card you registered with us has failed to authorize.'

Michael scoffs, 'What? Try it again.'

'It automatically tries three times, sir. As you know, when you pull up to the barrier with your car, it reads your number plate and checks you out. I'm afraid this time it was unable to authorize your payments.'

'That's ridiculous,' Michael bellows, 'I have never had this here, or anywhere for that matter.'

The receptionist smiles skilfully, 'That's true, sir. Your record of payments is exemplary. Do you have another card I could try?'

Michael sighs and shakes his head but nonetheless produces another card from his wallet. He watches with a face full of arrogance and indignation, but in truth, his chest is tightening. He's been watching for months as the numbers in his bank balance have become smaller and smaller, to the point where it has only been his credit that has been maintaining his appearance of stability.

If those have gone -

'I'm afraid that has also declined, sir.'

The words are a punch to the chest, but he keep his composure and whilst fumbling his phone from his pocket, shoots back, 'This is absurd. I am furious. I have never been so embarrassed. Your general manager will be hearing from me.'

'Sir, I do need a payment - '

'I know! Just wait!' he shouts. His voice echoes through the lobby, blessedly empty.

Dialling, he presses the phone to his ear, swallows his pride and speaks when the call is picked up, 'Yes, it me. I'm still in the lobby.'

In the bar, Ian, his phone at his ear, turns around and locks eyes with Michael. Confusion is in them.

Michael, his teeth gritted in frustration, knows he is lucky to have Ian, but bitterly resents having to make this call.

He sucks it up, grits his teeth, and asks, 'Can you come down? I need your help.'

4

The sound of the strings are melodic and pure. The stone behind him reverberates the acoustics perfectly, projecting the music out into the air before him. It surrounds him, fills his world, becomes his world. Along with the pain.

His right hand is wrapped in a bandage, a white strap between fingers and thumb. A blotch of red sits both in the centre of the palm and the top of the hand. The fingers tremble as they oscillate vertically, barely gripping the pick as it snags the strings in time to the music in Travis's head.

The haunting melody of *Red Right Hand* echoes across the expansive market square, drawing looks from the passing pedestrian traffic running left to right. Most notice the noise, but a few break their stride to listen in recognition of the song. Fewer still drop coins into the guitar case at his feet.

After six hours of relentless playing, Travis had noticed a trend and had played Red Right Hand every few songs, favouring it over *O Children* and *Where The Wild Roses Grow* due to its identifiable nature.

Smell what sells. And he needed to sell.

Shit, his hand is killing him.

It throbs painfully with every strum of the strings, a sharp ache that pulls on the tendons of his hand and all the way to his forearm. With every strike, the pick is becoming looser and looser in his grip.

And the rain has started. Only drizzle at first, but in the few minutes since it began, the drops have become thicker, heavier. The hoods have come up, the umbrellas are unsheathed. No one is listening to him now. They are hurrying on, their destination more important to them than standing in the street, listening to a strained rendition of a TV show's opening title music.

Travis isn't even singing. He had started, but he is tired and stressed. His voice isn't up to it.

Pain.

He has no hood. The rain has drenched his red hair and

it hangs across his face, water dripping into his eyes, as they drift along the length of the guitar neck to where a photograph is clipped.

He stares at it. It has served to inspire him this day. Not only due to its poignant content, but the fact that it saved him from further injury.

This is the second time I have had to deal with Matt on this subject. Baxter's voice echoes in Travis's mind. *But this is your first offence.*

Strike One.

Travis plays through the discomfort, eyes locked on the photograph.

Just another half an hour. Town is getting quiet, there'll be no more point after that anyway, or at least it'll be the wrong sort of crowd. Loud, drunk, obnoxious people.

He'll be more at risk of losing what little he has made than making any more.

Baxter had seen the photo. Travis had told him what it showed. There had been mercy.

I'll do only one hand. But you make this right, or it will be Strike Two next.

The pick drops from Travis's fingers. The music ceases suddenly, awkwardly, mid-verse. This does, of course, get people's attention.

Travis, grimacing under his long, soaking hair, drops to

one knee to pick it up.

Enough.

He rubs his hand carefully, trying to massage the pain away. It doesn't work. Just makes it worse.

Placing the acoustic guitar by his side, he uses his good hand to scoop the selection of coins out of the case and count them.

£18.36.

Six hours for that. He is sure there should have been more. There is a five pound note in there, several pound coins but a lot of silver.

Is it enough?

It would have to be. He is out of time.

Travis shoves the money into the pocket of his leather jacket and rests the guitar carefully in its case. He clicks it shut, hoists it onto his shoulder, and sets off across the square.

*

The Tesco on Maid Marian Way is still open. A beacon of bright light on an otherwise dark main road. Travis steps through the automatic doors, ignoring the second glance from the blue clad security guard, and starts up the first aisle.

His stomach grumbles, his mouth is parched.

Running his eyes over the shelves at the snacks section, he snatches up a *tuna crunch* sandwich and finds a can of own brand energy drink. He then begins searching the other aisles, dodging around languorous students having emerged sluggishly from their inner city dorms to hunt for high-sugar, low cost snacks. At the end of the second aisle, the security guard is watching him.

Prick.

Travis looks away from him and scans the shelves. Where is it? He saw it in the other Tesco. It must be here somewhere.

He turns away from the watchful, judgemental eyes, goes down the next passageway, and sees what he is looking for.

A narrow section at the end of the aisle; a cardboard display emblazoned with the words *Valentine's Day, 14th February*. Generally, it annoyed him to see commercial holidays advertised so early, more than three weeks in this case, but for now, it suited his purpose. He knew what he needed. This was the only place that he could get it.

Travis takes the small brown bear off the shelf and holds it in his hands, studying it. It's small, but it has a cute face and large button-eyes. In its arms is a large, red love heart that says *Forever Yours* in curling script.

It will do.

He turns the tag to see the price.

£17.99. Fucking hell!

He thought it said £7.99 in the other shop. Dammit, he must have misread it. He can't afford that.

Cursing, he slams it back on the shelf.

It sits there, staring back at him with unseeing eyes. It knows that he needs it. Travis can't turn up with nothing and ask what he needs to ask.

If he buys it, it leaves him 37 pence to eat with.

Shit. Is he hungrier or thirstier?

Travis grabs the bear back off the shelf, and tosses the sandwich and the can onto another random shelf. Returning to the snacks aisle, he grabs a bag of *Frazzles* for 35 pence.

He turns to head for the tills and stops. Someone is watching him from the end of the shop. It is not the security guard.

Travis freezes. Tries to see if he recognizes the man, momentarily unsure if he has seen him before, at the derelict warehouse or elsewhere. His hand starts to hurt again, a reminder.

The man's face is familiar. Average height, white, broad shouldered and bearded, with a deep, badly healed cut on his upper lip. He looks like a common or garden thug. Travis questions if he is being paranoid. The only people he distinctly remembers from that night were Matt and the drill-wielding Baxter.

He steps away from the snacks and wanders as casually as he can along the back of the shop, glancing surreptitiously down the aisles. The man has not followed.

He exhales with shaky breaths and walks to the tills. Choosing the self-checkout due to the embarrassment of having to pay with so much change, he scans his two items. The process of paying takes a few minutes and the machine sucks six hours of his day, one coin at a time. The loss of the note pains him the most.

Finally, it spits out a receipt. Travis feels he should keep it to assuage the obvious suspicions of the security guard. He tucks the bear under his arms, rips the bag of crisps open, and shoves a handful of the bacon-flavoured shards into his mouth.

He almost spits them back out. The bearded man is right in front of him, staring at him, smiling warmly.

Travis can do nothing but try to chew. His mouth is suddenly even drier than it already was. He is unable to say anything.

The man nods a greeting, 'Alright, Travis? How's the

hand?'

Travis, too stunned to say anything, simply stares, and the man puts a hand on his shoulder, squeezing it tightly, 'Good to see you, bro.'

The man with the cut lip gently pushes Travis, guiding him towards the door, while staying where he is.

Travis walks past the guard, who watches him, but is forgotten by the object of his interest. Back in the cold, wet air, Travis walks slowly away from the bright doorway.

The man is standing, taking a pack of on-offer biscuits from a shelf. He looks over his shoulder, waves affably.

Finally clearing his mouth of the dry food, Travis turns away and keeps walking, his heart hammering in his chest. The man's presence was a message from Baxter.

You are being watched.

*

The bar is still heaving as Camilla comes back down the stairs, letting the heavy door drift to close behind her. In truth, it is even busier. Any open space on the floor has now been filled in with bodies jostling for room; to maintain the circle of the group, to ease towards the bar, which cannot be seen at all.

Camilla's head has been whirling since Cassandra left.
It's happened. It's actually happening. It's going to happen.
The thrill of the prospect is almost too much to keep concealed. She wants to jump and shout and hug people, but then she'd have to confess why she is so happy, and *no-one* would understand.
'What the fuck?' they would say. 'Are you mental? Are you a psycho? What kind of bitch sells her baby?'
Nobody would understand. Nobody could. Well, some people could, but they'd never admit it.
Do you hate your baby?
God no. She most certainly does not hate her baby; that's the absolute truth, but it is also the problem. At least hate would be an emotion. At least then, she would feel *something* towards it.
Camilla had held the baby for a few minutes when the door had shut behind Cassandra, leaving her alone in her flat. She had pulled the tiny person to her chest, drank in how he fit neatly in her arms, inhaled his scent, gazed at the pure innocence of his returning stare.
Nothing.
Camilla had seen Cassandra's face as she had held the baby. She had visibly melted. She was a strong, successful woman who did nothing that she did not want to, whose outward projection of herself was measured and

controlled, and yet all that composure had dissolved in a second. Camilla saw what that woman saw; in a heartbeat, her whole future sprawled out before her. Hopes, dreams, passions... legacy. Everything she had ever wanted and would ever want lay in her arms, its tiny hands holding her finger.

When Camilla held him, her only thought was that her arms were getting tired.

She had moved into her bedroom, where a small cot sat beside the unmade double bed, one of the barred sides down. Placing the baby on its back, and tucking the swaddling blanket tightly under its back, she sat cross legged on the bed and picked up her phone to mindlessly drag her finger across her social life.

It was a good baby, by all accounts. Sure, it cried when it was hungry, or needed a nappy change, or winding, but all it needed in order to sleep was leaving alone. She had found that out the hard way. Hours and hours of pacing whilst it wailed so hard she was sure it was going to pass out, only for it to stop after ten minutes because she'd put it down and left the room for a break.

Self-soothing, Camilla had heard it was called. After that, she simply plonked it down, made sure it was safe enough and sat by whilst it cooed itself to sleep.

Had she told her friends about the baby, they would

have been wonderfully jealous.

After the standard ten minutes, the baby had indeed drifted off. Camilla eased the side of the cot up, not that it was going anywhere, and watched it for a moment.

Its tiny chest rose and fell under the soft blanket, its eyes closed, bottle-puckered lips slightly apart.

Beautiful.

Camilla appreciated the aesthetic properties of her offspring. She simply didn't feel it. She didn't feel anything.

No, that wasn't true. She did feel one thing.

Resentment.

In the bar, Camilla pushes her way through the people towards the bar. Brandon and Linnea glance up at her with irritation as they battle the relentless onslaught, and even Sam is there, busy tossing spirits into a tall glass and sloshing in fruit juice and ice. He spots Camilla and jerks his head beckoning her, wanting her to take over.

He finishes serving his customer just as Camilla manages to push by the young glass collector at the end of the counter. Already, patrons' eyes have locked onto Camilla, vying to be next.

Sam pushes his way out before Camilla can get in, and says sharply, 'That took bloody long enough.'

'He wouldn't settle.'

Sam snorts, 'Don't bullshit a bullshitter. That kid's a diamond.'

Camilla shoots him a sharp look, 'Yeah, well, won't be your problem for much longer will it.'

She shoves past him to the bar, but he catches her elbow as she passes. It's a gentle movement, without violence, almost fatherly. Camilla doesn't look at him, but he leans close enough so that he does not have to shout above the music.

'That's not fair. I do a lot for you.'

Camilla shrugs, 'And you get a lot back from me, Sam.'

'Camilla, it's not even a done deal yet. We're weeks away, months, probably. I'll make sure you're both okay long before I sign anything. I've promised you this.'

She looks back at him, 'Fat lot of good a promise is when I'm living on the streets.'

Sam rolls his eyes and shakes his large head, 'Fuck me, Camilla, you're so god-damned dramatic. Do you even listen when I talk?'

A voice from the crowd shouts, 'Excuse me, you serving, love?'

Camilla pulls her arm free and steps away, leaving Sam without a reply. She knows she is being pig-headed, and Sam thinks he is being reasonable, but she couldn't give a shit. It makes her furious when she thinks about it.

A Kiss At Midnight

Her blood genuinely feels like it is boiling. She hates him for what he's doing, for making her hate him.

Sam *had* done a lot for her, not just babysitting for a few hours while she worked when the baby was awake, but she had lived for nearly two years in the flat upstairs and paid very little open rent. Sam took some out of her wages each month, but it was a flexible amount, comparatively small and dependent on what her other outgoings were. She paid her own utilities; they were her responsibility.

Camilla serves the first group. Some obscure and complicated cocktail, the ingredients and method long since committed to memory, three Peroni and four Jäger-bombs. She completes the order on autopilot.

Her flat is the single best thing in her life. She knows she was lucky to get it and makes sure she appreciates it. Camilla had worked hard to furnish it how she wanted; simple, elegant, modern. It is everything she dreamed of as a teenager in her parents' house. Better. She had been twenty-four, with a secure flat in the middle of the city centre, where she could stagger five minutes from any bar in town to her own bed, with anyone she pleased. And, in the morning, roll out of that bed for a choice of dozens of breakfasts. She could eat a different meal in a different place for a month without repeat. All that Sam asked in return, other than his reduced rent, was that she be on hand to fill in on shifts for staff who didn't turn up, or take deliveries and a hundred other little tasks because she lived upstairs,

And most of all, she was beholden to nobody.

But that had changed.

Nine months ago, her perfect little world had been slowly crumbling at the same speed that her belly had swollen up. And she loathes the person who took it from her.

The customers take their drinks and, for a moment, the bar clears, allowing a fleeting glimpse across the room, to the door, where someone is stood looking at her.

Camilla shakes her head. God, when that *twat* enters her head, she can't get rid of him. Moving to the next customer, pushing the thought of him out her mind, she throws another look at the door and freezes.

No. It really is him. He is here.

Fucking Travis.

5

The Mercedes floats up onto the driveway with barely a whisper, and stops behind the white Range Rover already parked there. Michael does not get out immediately. He sits, hands gripping the wheel tightly, running the evening through his mind, reassuring himself that every decision that he has made was the right one.

Michael has never doubted himself. Another of his qualities; a steadfast confidence that he always knows best. He is always right.

The incident with the hotel payment has changed things, however. In his line of work, Michael has had a number of close calls, but it has always worked out for him.

He has never been this close to the wire before. Now, he feels doubt.

It has shaken his confidence a little. Only a little, but even a little is still a one hundred percent increase on the norm.

He gets out into the rain and locks the car with a click as he walks away, along the path that runs up the lawn to the house. It is a property typical to Edwalton, an elegant new build less than six years old. Overpriced and under-sized, its purpose was to demonstrate stature; a declaration of the owner's standing. It didn't matter that at the other end of the county, one could get three bigger houses for almost the same cost; there would be no statement.

I am affluent. I have power. Envy me.

Michael unlocks the black front door and enters the long hallway, wiping his shoes on the mat. A few lamps are lit, one in the hall, one in the living room on the left. A light is coming from the far end, blue, from the under-counter lighting.

There is the scent of rose oil and other such smells, drifting down the stairs on the same air that carries the sound of soothing strings. A tinkling of water moving. A flicker of candlelight.

Michael shuts the door quietly, not wanting to alert her to his presence yet, then hangs his coat on the hat stand before wandering towards the kitchen.

It is a large space at the back of the house that comprises of the generous kitchen, the over-large white dining table with six chairs, and small, plush seating area. It looks out on the garden through a wall of glass that can be slid away, opening the wall entirely.

Michael makes for the cupboard by the sofas, taking out a bottle of brandy and a glass. He tosses a small measure in, throws it into his mouth before decanting another. This time he simply holds it and looks out across the room.

He has always liked this room the best. The other rooms in the house are big enough, but this one really does make a statement. It's impressive. It invites comment from visitors. It does its job. It would be a major disappointment to lose it.

The house so far is secure. Fully paid for. If things did indeed continue to go south, it would be the last thing to go.

A tightening in his chest. Shit, that hotel issue is really affecting him. He isn't used to it.

Then, as if the universe is listening and wants to weigh in on his inner conversation, his phone rings. It's Ian.

Michael swallows the brandy and answers, 'Let me have it.'

'They made another offer.'

Michael sits on the arm of the sofa, silently exhaling, expelling the pressure in his chest. His voice however remains casual, 'I see. Good.'

'Three-eighty.'

Michael offers no more than a grunt in reply and Ian is quickly in his ear, 'Is that all you have to say, Michael? Hmm. We got lucky. They really want this land. I don't want to say too much but whoever they are, they clearly need somewhere to sink some money quickly and quietly. We can't pass this up.'

'Ian, it's my property. I'll do with it exactly what I feel.' Michael replies. He knows he is being a dick and loves it. He feels like himself again. Confident. Correct.

'Michael, please. Let me call them back and accept.' Ian goes on. 'They don't want to play games. They want a deal. These are their words.'

'I'm not playing games, Ian. I'm doing what I do best. I said no to three-twenty-five and they added fifty-five K on,' Michael says. 'Why, after all these years, do you still doubt me?'

'Because you've lost most of your business in less than a year, Michael. That's why!'

A low blow, regardless of its truth. Michael says nothing, simply standing up and pacing to the kitchen, taking the time to formulate his answer. Ian had never said this, at least never so bluntly. It didn't matter that he was worried; he was getting above his station.

Michael replies, 'You need to wind your neck in, Ian. You're an accountant. I pay you to look after my money. At the end of the day our relationship is professional, not personal.'

No reply, then Ian says, his tone level, 'Yes, and I would like to continue to be paid by you, but that's not going to happen if you fuck this up too.'

Ian had never said fuck. Not ever in his life, so far as Michael knew.

Michael taps his glass on the counter top.

It's Ian who breaks the silence, 'If you don't take this, Michael, I'm out. I have to be.'

Michael still says nothing.

'Michael, you there?'

'I'm here.'

Ian sighs deeply, 'They say you have until midnight to agree, or they'll take their money elsewhere. Let me make the call.'

Michael clears his throat, 'I don't like being over a barrel, Ian. You know that.' An even deeper sigh from the phone, cut short by Michael. 'I'll call them myself. I'll accept the offer, but I'll do it in my time. That clear?'

*

After hanging up on Ian, Michael pours himself another brandy. He needs it for the next conversation.

Glass in hand, he heads up the stairs, towards the sound of Ludovico Einaudi's strings and the ever increasing aroma of scented candles burning.

Ian had agreed that he would wait for Michael to call them, to make them sweat, but if it got too late, Ian was going to make the call on his behalf.

At the top of the stairs, Michael can see the door at the end of the landing open a crack. The soft flicker of candle light plays along the neutral walls and framed paintings that were produced en masse but limited to those who could afford them.

The sorrowful whining of strings, a piano's melodic yield, both gentle and hard, both leading and allowing to be led, combine in Einaudi's *Walk* composition.

It is one of her favourites, and Michael has to admit that he is drawn to this piece also. It is one of the few things they shared, that they agreed upon.

Michael pushes the door open. The bathroom is long.

A Kiss At Midnight

Another great feature, but not original. They had ripped out the bland, catalogue-bought suite that came with the house, and designed their own. A grey-tiled wet-room on the right, a pair of his-and-hers mirrors on the left, and at the end, a deep roll top bath set against a tall window.

Candles are placed around the bathtub, music coming from a blue-tooth speaker hidden away somewhere.

Michael crosses to the bath and sits on the edge of one end, crosses his knee over the other, his brandy loose in his hand. He looks down, studies her, and smiles warmly.

Cassandra, her face moist with the heat from the water, looks back up at him. Her hair is tied up and stray hair hangs loose and wet by her ears. Her shoulders sit above the water; bubbles cover her but for the tops of her knees. She doesn't smile, but it looks like she almost is. It is something she has always done and makes it impossible for Michael to read her.

She speaks first, 'How did it go?'

'They made an offer', Michael replies, his eyes looking at her knees, his mind wandering.

'A good one?'

'It is now.'

Cassandra nods, lifts her hands out of the water, and begins to run a nail file swiftly across her fingertips. 'Are we good?'

Michael grins, 'Of course we are.'

He sips his brandy and looks at her. She is wearing the necklace he bought her for her birthday two years before; a bizarre design that only an archetypal straight male could pick out, but obviously expensive.

'Aren't you going to ask me about my evening?' Cassandra asks in her low, almost husky voice, without looking away from her nails.

'I was waiting for you,' he replies, receiving a dubious look from her. 'How was it?'

Cassandra stops filing and looks at him directly. A genuine smile spreads across her face. 'I fell in love, Michael. Truly and deeply. I want him.'

Michael nods slowly, sips his brandy, his expression neutral. 'I see. Um, okay. Are you sure? Do you not want to... look at others?'

'What the hell are you talking about, Michael?' Cassandra says sharply, 'I'm not browsing the fucking Argos catalogue. This is a baby. A person. And besides that, do you happen to know many people who are selling their children?'

'Cassie, there are other ways –'

'Adoption, Michael?' she retorts, 'Do you not listen to a word I say? I do not want to *adopt* a child, I want one of my own.'

She continues to work on her nails, 'The baby is unregistered. We'll go to your friend, Doctor Flynn, get him to draw up some records declaring and backdating my pregnancy -'

'Cassie, I don't know if John will... it doesn't work like that...'

'Then make it work like that.'

Michael doesn't reply. He finishes the brandy sharply, thinking.

'If you didn't want me to have this, then why on earth did you introduce me to Camilla?'

There is no answer. Just silence and a blank stare.

Cassandra looks at him with that unreadable expression and suddenly rises up from the water until its level drops to her navel. She reaches out, above her head to a shelf and takes down a sponge, before sinking back into the concealment of the bubbles.

Michael's eyes follow her, locked several inches below her face.

Cassandra dips the sponge into the water, takes it out, and wipes down her neck with it, 'I want that baby, Michael.'

Michael doesn't reply. He is still looking at the bubbles. Water parts and Cassandra's left knee moves, rises, extends, and becomes longer until her calf and foot project out from the bath.

Michael watches her foot lower and drop onto his thigh. A wet patch spreads across the trouser beneath the leg, but he does not stir, as if movement might frighten away the skittish creature. He transfers the glass to his right hand and with his left, he reaches out.

His palm grazes the damp skin. Cassandra watches him as he runs it down her shin. His eyes flick up to her, trying to read her. The hand slides off the leg and into the water. She doesn't move. Water rises up, along Michael's arm, soaking his shirtsleeve as it sinks lower, moving towards Cassandra, until his elbow is submerged.

'Stop.'

Cassandra's tone is firm.

Michael's arm sinks further.

'I said... *stop*,' she says again, no louder, but there is an inarguable finality to her voice.

Michael's lips are dry. He licks them, 'Cassie... please.'

'Take your hand away.'

'It's been so long, I...'

'*Away.*'

Biting his lips, as if the movement is painful, Michael slowly draws his hand away, above the waterline. Water pours from his saturated, discoloured shirt. Cassandra's leg shifts, rises from him, drops silently back into the bath. Her knee re-joins the other.

'I want that baby, Michael,' she states slowly, 'And when you get me what I want, I will give you what you want. That is the deal we made. There is no other.'

Michael turns away, leaning on his knee with his elbow; wet arm to dry leg. He rubs his head, running his finger through his hair thoughtfully, before saying, 'A hundred grand?'

'That's what you said.'

Michael stands quickly, fists clenched, taking a few steps away, 'I'm going out again.'

'To see Ian?'

A pause.

Michael shrugs and bustles out abruptly, anger in his heart and desire in his belly.

6

It had taken the best part of thirty minutes for Travis to get to the bar, and all Camilla could do was wait for him. She serves person after person, always keeping her eyes on him as he patiently waits his turn. Dozens of bottles of beers, litres of spirits and their accompanying mixers, wines and cocktails, even the rare soft drink, all prepared and handed out. With every drink proffered, Travis takes a step towards her.

He never takes his gaze off her.

Finally, he is there, leaning over the bar in his sodden coat, his stupid guitar case slung across his back. She studies him, comparing this face that stares back at her to the one she used to know. It is narrower, the eyes darker, sunk into his pallid skin, and his ginger hair seems thinner too.

Camilla takes an order from a tall guy and his girlfriend, and sets out collecting their order. She glances over at Linnea and Sam, both serving, works out who is next, and when they'd finish their orders.

It's no use. Travis is her next customer in line. Even if she skips him, so that Linnea has to serve him, he'd only ask for her.

Maybe she can get one of the doormen to get rid of him, or Sam. Sam would definitely eject him if Camilla claims that he is bothering her. She 'doesn't have to tell him who Travis is.

But Travis would declare it to Sam. Even if Sam 'doesn't believe him outright, questions would be asked.

She has to face him. Find out what he wants, then tell him to fuck off.

A pair of gin lemonades. Money taken.

Travis looks at her with a blend of nervousness and happiness, 'Hi, Cammy.'

Only *he* had ever called her Cammy.

'What do you want, Travis?' she replies curtly, 'I'm working.'

He is clearly expecting the attitude; doesn't seemed fazed. Camilla is waiting for the anger, the rage, the moral high horse.

'You look beautiful.'

It takes her aback, but she repeats the question, 'What do you want?'

'You know what I want.'

Camilla doesn't reply. Lets him lead the conversation, to guard against offering any information. He might not even know. His sudden appearance might be unrelated.

'I want to see my son.'

Shit.

Camilla's vision suddenly blurs, blackness around the edges. There is a pressure in her head. She inhales, grips the bar. Feels like she might fall over. Why now? Why tonight? Why couldn't he have turned up tomorrow?

Suddenly he leans over the bar, touches her hand. It jerks her back to the present and she looks down at the intrusion, seeing the red-spotted bandage. She almost asks what happened to it; old habits die hard.

Camilla pulls her hand away, looks him in the eye and steels herself, 'Don't know what you're talking about.'

Travis taps his hand on the bar, then reaches inside his coat, removes the photograph that he has pinned to the neck of his guitar all day; the one that saved his other hand from mutilation.

Camilla looks at it, inwardly gasps at its familiarity. A

fuzzy black and white image, framed inside an inverted triangle, a vague bean shaped object. Camilla's name captioned at the top, a date, a number, the name of the maternity department.

Travis shakes the photograph at her, 'Daniella got in touch, Cammy. Why didn't you tell me?'

Daniella. Her fucking interfering, self-righteous sister. Camilla's anger must be clear on her face because Travis says, 'She thought I should know that I had a kid. It's only right, Cammy. Fair, to me and to... him.'

He jostles the image to make his point.

Camilla says nothing. Her heart is pounding, her mind cluttered with venomous retorts, crowding to the front of her mind like people at this bar. Each one wanting to be served first, pushing and shoving, and demanding that they are the most important of the group.

'You deserve nothing!' The words are out. Confirmation. Travis grins and leans over the bar. Beside him, another patron is becoming annoyed at the long conversation and gives both Camilla and Travis a succession of disgruntled looks.

Camilla, realizing that only seconds into the conversation that she has been dreading, hoping would never come, had still prepared for, it has already gone awry.

'It doesn't matter anyway, Travis,' she bellows hurriedly, 'because you're not seeing him. You're not his dad.'

'Daniella says I am!'

'Daniella doesn't know shit!'

A good response. This might work. Travis had always been a flake; if anything ever got too difficult, he'd back out.

Travis frowns, holding something else, 'He is mine, Cammy. I know it. I know you. You're a lot of things, but you ain't a cheat. He's mine. Please, just let me see him. Let's just talk.'

Then, as if it proves some sort of further point, he places the Valentine's bear on the counter-top, 'I brought this for him.'

Camilla scoffs, unable to resist the smile; the origin of which she cannot place, as either derision or amusement. She looks at the pathetic little item and recognises it from Tesco.

Travis grins and cocks his head apologetically, 'It's all I could afford.'

Camilla shrugs. She needs to get rid of him, before everything comes undone, 'I don't want you here, Travis. Fuck off, or I'll have you removed.'

'Cammy, please –'

Camilla raises her hand, waves at the doors, at the

bouncers there. One of them catches sight of her. She turns the wave to a point, directs it at the top of Travis's head.

Travis looks around at the approaching doorman, and sees what she has done. Panic takes over his face and he leans over the bar, 'No, Cammy, please! I need your help, I'm in trouble.'

Camilla sneers, 'I knew there'd be something else. You are a selfish prick. You don't care about your son. That's why I didn't want anything to do with you.' It's a complete lie, but it works in the scenario.

'No, I swear. Daniella called me, told me, and sent me the photo. I was on my way but... something happened! Please, Cammy, I need your help or I'm -' He holds up his hand, and pulls the bandage off, revealing the damage beneath. Spots of wet blood splash onto the counter with the movement. People groan and step away, swearing and cursing.

Camilla stares at the wound. A deep hole, almost half an inch wide between the tendons in the back of his hand, the meat inside torn up and twisted, oozing fluid. It jars her, makes her misplace her resolve.

Poor guy. She has grown to hate him, fed that hate for nearly a year, but had loved him deeply once.

No. That was history. He was no longer a part of her

life. He is an obstacle to be overcome.

The bouncer's hands grab at his shoulder and neck, pulling him.

'Camilla! This is only the start if they don't get their money!'

Camilla shrugs as convincingly as she can, 'Of course it's money! It's always money with you!'

Travis is overcome by the far larger man, yanked away. 'Cammy! I only have ' Then he is out of earshot, hidden behind the bass of the music and finally obscured by bodies.

No longer able to see him, she lets out a gasp of pent up tension. Her eyes fall onto the bar top, at the white paper there. She snatches it up; it has a phone number scrawled on it in Travis's childish script. She flips it; it is the sonogram.

Camilla slips it into her pocket, out of sight, before anyone sees it, and turns away from the bar and the crowd, who bray at her in acrimonious symphony with her own chaotic thoughts.

'Camilla?' It is Sam, looking at her with concern, 'You alright?'

She looks up, nods, and his reply is curt, 'Fucking serve then!'

Her chest tightens with frustration. To her, Sam and

Travis might as well be working together to fuck up her life; in the last twelve months both had conspired against her, sought to take away everything she had, make her life a thick swamp of the unwanted and underserved problems that she now waded though.

She needs out.

She needs it now.

Camilla barks back at him in a manner that none of her colleagues would ever dare to, 'I need a minute!'

Without waiting for a reply, she turns and pushes her way through people to the quietest part of the bar, and takes up her phone to dial furiously.

It is answered quickly. Camilla speaks rapidly, not even bothering to try and sound calm, 'I want to do this tonight. When can you bring the money?'

*

Cassandra puts the phone down and cannot contain herself. She allows herself the luxury of a little whoop of joy and twirls on the soft carpet of the bedroom. She knows she looks like a girlish idiot, but for the briefest of moments, she does not care.

The silk dressing gown floats as she spins until she is too dizzy and flops onto the satin bed sheets, sighing happily.

A Kiss At Midnight

It is a feeling beyond mere excitement; more a state of pure contentment; it is a sensation that Cassandra has long pursued and now cannot entirely believe is within her reach.

A feeling of perfect wholeness. A baby. Her child.

On the bed, she finds her hand pressed against her belly. It is not the ability to bear a child that makes a mother, but the ability to raise one. And Cassandra is ready, has been ready for a long time, and the fact that she could not carry her own was long a cause of great suffering. In time, she had accepted that this was her lot, the hand she had been dealt and had made peace with it.

Made peace and grabbed an opportunity that presented itself with both hands. She was not going to let go.

She stands up, grabbing her phone as she does, and dials. A full-length mirror on the door of the giant wardrobe allows her to gaze at herself while the phone is ringing. She pictures herself with a baby in her arms, both in matching Analogias outfits, a Silver Cross pushchair by her waist, and a Victoria Beckham changing bag hanging off the handles.

Perfection.

'Cassandra?' The phone is answered cautiously.

'I want to meet,' Cassandra replies coolly.

A moment of quiet, of processing, then 'Is he there?'

'No. He's gone out again, and not with you, I'm guessing.'

'Of course he's not. For goodness' sake!' A sigh, 'I'll come over.'

Cassandra shakes her head, 'No, I'll see you at the Embankment in thirty.'

7

In movies, when someone is ejected from a drinking establishment by bouncers, they are gripped by the collar and the belt, and then propelled like a sack into a pile of waiting bins or boxes. The reality is considerably more undignified; the grip on the collar is replaced by a firm, rough hand, clasped around the back of the neck, and instead of the belt, an arm twisted painfully across the shoulder blade.

Instead of an '*and don't you come back,*' delivered in a raspy, New York Brooklyn accent, Travis receives, 'Now fuck off, you scrawny little cunt,' before being shoved off the pavement into the road.

His trainers splash into the puddle collecting by the

kerbstones, soaking his feet through, and his semi-defiant look back at his aggressor only results in said person taking another two steps after him.

Travis, jerking his guitar case back onto his shoulder, holds up his hands to show deference, and steps away, heading away from the bar. Rain lashes down on him, as the bouncer retreats to the shelter of the doorway to watch him go.

Pulling his collar up, Travis walks towards St. Peter's Square, staying on the road until a passing car forces him back onto the pavement on the same side as the bar. Glancing back to make sure he wasn't going to further aggravate the bouncer, Travis can see A Bar called Cafe's red neon sign flickering in the rain; its crimson glow now reflected in the water on the road.

That was it. He only had one play and he had fucked it up.

His head bowed, he slows his pace, dropping the Valentine's bear on the ground. There is nowhere for him to go now. No reason to hurry out of the rain; the discomfort of being wet will be nothing compared to his fate when Baxter finds him again.

He wonders what time it is. How long he has left. Doesn't check. It's pointless.

Travis stops and leans against the metal railing of the

church. He feels drained. Wishes that he could just go to sleep now, drift off and never wake up. He presses his dripping forehead against the fence and forces the sound of the screaming drill out of his mind.

Thinks of the baby. The boy he has never met. His son. The sonogram gives no indication of what he might look like. It's almost conceptual. It is the idea of his son, intangible and theoretical. True, Travis is desperate for money, but even if Camilla cannot help him with that, if she had at least let him see his boy, that might have given him the strength with which to face the drill again.

He scoffs at himself. With the right motivation, people can convince themselves of anything that suits their current purpose.

Why hadn't Camilla told him that she was pregnant? That would have changed everything. He would not have moved down to London, would not have tried that ill-fated venture and gotten involved with Baxter. He would have stayed, made it work with Camilla somehow, and raised their son together. Here, in their tiny flat above a bar where they had shared so many laughs.

Despite the downpour, in that moment, he is enjoying a lazy summer sun, about to set over the rooftops. Sitting with Camilla snuggled into his arm against the slight chill, the smell of her shampoo in his head, the taste of her on the cigarette they share on the backstairs of the bar...

Then he is back in the rain, but he has pushed himself away from the wall with renewed purpose. Travis looks across his shoulder at the bouncers in the doorway. A group of students are pushing their way inside, held back as the doormen insist on seeing their IDs, of whom only half have them.

They are busy.

His memory a map, Travis walks quickly back up the road towards the bar until he is past the railings, sliding along the windows of the estate agents next door to the bar.

There it is. A narrow alleyway that splits the two buildings, guarded by a green gate, a mesh fence above it to prevent anyone climbing over.

There is no need to climb; the gate is never locked, just stiff due to swelling of the wood. At least, it never used to be locked. A sharp knock with his shoulder and it should swing open.

Travis looks at the bouncers. Half of the students are inside now, the remaining couple still debating knowledge of their birthdays and questionable resemblances to the photos on their IDs.

Still distracted for a few more seconds. The noise of him

charging the door with his shoulder would get their attention. If he got it wrong, they would be on him. He literally had one chance. Even if it 'isn't locked and it 'doesn't open on the first try, that thug would be all over him again.

Travis presses his shoulder against the wood, grips the metal handle and braces himself. He moves away and, both pulling himself to the gate and pushing with his feet, he throws himself into it.

A bang. A creak. A squeal.

It gives way.

Trying to keep the momentum, and in so doing, tripping over his sodden trainers and bashing the guitar on the narrow opening, he falls inside.

He closes the gate behind him and waits, breathing hard. There is no noise from the other side. No footsteps, no talking. Only the hiss of the rain on the pavement.

Travis moves away from the gate as silently as he can, stepping lightly across the grimy floor of the alley. He remembers it reaches the end and takes a sharp right turn to another gate, this one locked, that leads out to the back of the church. Before that, there is a set of metal stairs, historically a fire escape, the top of which isa perfect place to share a cigarette. The door there leads into the back of the flat, to where the old storeroom was split into two bedrooms. Travis is sure the smaller of them is where his son will be.

Excitement propels him up the stairs, and he ignores the clatter and squeak he makes as he climbs. The door there is wide and thick, with a solid, protruding handle and a keyhole.

He grabs the handle and pulls.

It doesn't move even a little. A solid fire door that requires a key. A key he had never had.

'Fuck!' he screams at the top of his lungs, 'Fuck...' He bangs his head against the door, deadening the excruciating failure. His son is just the other side, only feet away. Less than the length of his arms.

The rain hammers down around him, filling his world with noise.

This is it. He had tried, but there is nothing more he can do.

'Bit of trouble there, bro?'

The voice echoes up from the gloom of the alley beneath him. Gulping, Travis reaches out to the railings, looks down, and his crippling sense of defeat is doubled.

*

Camilla bursts into the flat. The single *minute* that she

had promised Sam as she sent the text had turned out to be a lie.

She tries to slam the heavy door behind her, but the door-closer cushions it, slowing it to a crawl. Snarling, she pushes it with all her weight, trying to create a satisfying bang to illustrate her fury, but it fights her. The resulting is a whoosh and slightly louder click than normal.

As trivial and arbitrary as it is, Camilla feels it is yet another thing that simply cannot go right for her. The faces of Sam, kicking her out of her home, and Travis, burdening her with his child, float before her.

She storms across the room, clutching at her hair, kicking over a nest of tables, bought proudly from Dunelm only the month before. The item crashes into the wall, creating the much desired crash.

Camilla stops. *Crap, what an idiot.* She listens. A sleepy whimper floats through from the back bedroom, but amounts to nothing. *Damn, that is a good baby.* Cassandra is getting a bargain; Camilla should have charged more.

Taking a few breaths, trying to calm herself and her shaking hands, she looks sadly down at the mess of tiny tables. One of the surfaces is scratched, another's leg is broken, snapped at the bolt. She really liked them. Had her eye on them for weeks before paying the high price for them.

A smile creeps out from the corner of her mouth and she shakes her head incredulously at herself. Her remorse at the broken furniture really was the definition of pointless.

She laughs loudly in the quiet of her flat.

Yeah, how stupid of her.

Camilla takes the bottle of vodka out of a cupboard, unscrews the lid, and takes a long drink. It nearly makes her gag as it burns her throat and hits her stomach, but it works. It cools her mind, takes the edge off the anxiety, and focuses her intent.

Tonight. All of it.

Fuck Travis. Fuck Sam.

Cassandra would be in in about an hour. Plenty of time to make her preparations.

Camilla takes the canvas changing-bag off the sofa. From a low cupboard, she snatches a handful of nappies, a pack of wipes and nappy bags, and shoves them in. Into the kitchen, where she pulls the bottle of formula milk that Sam had prepared for her earlier, stuffs it in too. She looks around, goes through a list in her head. What will Cassandra need to get her through the night? The bitch is loaded, assuming she hasn't already raided

Mothercare and bought half the store. She'll be fine with getting cots, pushchairs and the nursery furniture that she'd require. All Cassandra will need is things to get through the night; feeding and changing, that baby can sleep anywhere. It will be like sending him off for a sleep-over, that's all.

Zipping the bag and tossing it back on the sofa, she crosses to the window. The single armchair sits there, the real fir tree from Christmas pinned behind it. Thin red curtains frame the window that looks out over rain-drenched St. Peter's Gate and the bright windows of the posh homeware shop opposite.

She stares at it for a moment. Is she really going to do this?

Pulling the chair away, holding the tree up in place until it promises not to fall on her, she looks under it, at the wall. There is an electrical socket, an innocuous three-pin timer plugged into the front, the sort used by old people to make their lamps come on at certain times in the evening.

The plan is simple. Get rid of the baby and return to her life, as it was. Before the baby, before Travis. The money she'll get will be more than enough to get her abroad. She'll simply vanish. No one will look for her. No one cares.

But Sam is *taking* her home away from her. Camilla is going anyway, but Sam is forcing her hand. If this deal weren't happening, she'd be homeless and penniless with an infant. She'd be truly fucked, and Sam couldn't give a shit.

He'll give a shit now, though.

Camilla steps back into the kitchen, takes another quick mouthful of the spirit before taking a roll of tin foil out of a drawer. She crouches back in front of the socket and unrolls a stretch of foil, breaking it off and rolling it into a long wire.

Ensuring the plug is switched off at the wall, she threads one end of the foil into one of the bottom holes, making it tight so that it won't fall out again. Carefully, she twists the other end around one of the lowermost, dried branches of the fir tree. Needles fall off as she manipulates it, again making sure it is secure.

Swallowing, she runs through the logic of steps in her mind before touching the timer dial on the socket. It's nearly 10.30pm now; Cassandra will be here to collect the baby within the hour. In, pick it up, hand over the money, a few words of advice for the night, then Cassandra will leave by the backstairs and the alleyway. Camilla will go right after. There's nothing to pack. She can't, it would be suspicious once the authorities had picked through the ashes and found any suggestion of arson. By then, Camilla would be in another country. Even if they track her there, she'll have left there too.

A new life. Away from all the men who had tried to ruin this one.

The truth was, it had worked out well. If Sam wasn't evicting her, she would never had thought of doing this, but in so doing, it created the perfect distraction; confusion, and at least, a temporary explanation for the police.

Camilla looks at her work. When the dial reaches the set time, it will switch the socket on, allowing the current through, along the tin foil to the dried, oily branches. It will go up like a bonfire. She'd seen how quickly real Christmas trees catch on fire; it will become an inferno within seconds. The flat will be hell on earth within minutes.

She twists the dial, makes sure that she has just enough time to make the sale and get out before any more complications occur.

12.00am.

Satisfied, she switches the socket on and feels, suddenly and finally, in control.

That sensation fades rapidly at the sound of her door being firmly knocked on.

8

A firm hand on his shoulder, Travis is guided by the Cut Lip man up Exchange Walk, back towards Market Square. Ahead, he can see the carved stone lion statue he was standing beside long, long before. A couple stand there now; a middle-aged man in a geometrically patterned shirt, soaked through, and a short, round woman of a matching age, in thigh boots leaning against him, lips locked. At the top, a tram passes noisily and he is steered left, past the bank and through the door of the Joseph Else Wetherspoon's pub.

Travis's mouth is dry and the side of his head still hurts from where the man had punched him. Upon seeing him at the flat, Travis had to barrel down the stairs towards the other gate. It was, as expected, locked, and Cut Lip explained his displeasure at the pursuit physically.

The pub is over-warm, heat blasting down into the doorway from above, with shoulder-to-shoulder bodies standing in groups, drinks in hand, voices loud.

Travis is pushed through them, along the side of the bar, towards the back of the room. Past shrill gambling machines being pummelled by men who are never as skilled as they portray themselves to be, and crowded tables, heaped with glasses.

He looks around. Cut Lip has said nothing about where they are going, and Travis is as angry as he is scared. This isn't fair. His time isn't up yet.

'Back of the room, bro,' Cut Lip commands, 'Keep going.'

He shoves Travis and, for a second, Travis loses himself and shakes the man's grip loose. Infuriated by the cheek, the man grabs the back of Travis's neck and gives him a harder shove.

'Behave your-fucking-self, bro.'

Travis stops, turns around, 'Where are we going?'

'Back of the room, like I said,' Cut Lip replies curtly, with a hint of a mischievous smile, made more perverse by his cut. 'Your mate's come to see you.'

Mate? What mate?

Travis's heart leaps painfully. *Baxter? Surely not – please not him.*

Cut Lip nods in the direction they are going. Travis turns, following the look, and is taken aback. A hard push and Travis walks towards the table in the corner where another man, a copy of Travis's escort, is stood. Sat at the table is a man in his late thirties, dark hair with a grubby beard and eyes that droop at the sides.

Those eyes drift up to Travis as he approaches, and there is both hope and hatred in them.

Travis stands over him and looks down to see why this man is seated.

A wheelchair is positioned under the table. On the top of the newly bought denim covering the man's thighs, there is a tiny spot of blood seeping through the bandages below.

'Matt...'

It is all Travis can say. Sympathy, fear, shame and anger. He studies Matt's face. It is pale and withered, unfathomably tired. His lips, now thin lines, part, and he speaks with a croak, 'Travis, you fucking arsehole. Please tell me you have the money.'

Travis opens his mouth, shrugs his shoulders, and shakes his head, 'I was trying, Matt-'

Suddenly, the hand on his shoulder encourages him to sit down. Travis pulls out the chair and falls into it. Matt stares at him, but Travis cannot meet his gaze.

'I hate you,' Matt whispers, 'I really do fucking hate you.'

'Matt, come on - '

'Fuck your *come on*, you prick,' Matt spits, 'Look at me. Go on, fucking look at me!'

Travis glances up, but cannot maintain it, 'I'm sorry-'

Matt scoffs, takes a drink from the glass of water before him, and nods at his legs. 'I keep losing blood, you know. Won't clot. Wounds keep opening every time I move even a little bit. They won't give me stitches because they say there's no point.'

Travis gulps, 'Why?'

Matt shakes his head incredulously, 'You still have no real idea about what you're into, do you? I mean, you're lucky Baxter has a soft spot for kids. One fucking hand – Christ – you jammy fuck.'

He puts the glass down and holds up both of his own hands. On the back of each is a little circle, about half the size of a penny, a dome of healed skin. On his palms, the same.

Travis rubs his own hand, his own wound, self-consciously.

Matt coughs. 'What about this bird then? You seen her yet?'

Travis nods, frowning.

'And?'

'And nothing,' Travis replies, 'She'd barely even talk to me, and when I asked for money...'

Matt scoffs. 'Well, that's that then. We're both fucked. I mean, what a mess – getting into business with you is the worst thing I have ever done, Travis, and I've spent my life doing silly shit.'

'It was a good plan, Matt-'

'Yeah, it was a good, good plan. I agree,' Matt says, nodding. 'Simple and legitimate – it should have been the start of something, Trav. Something good. Something that helped us both get our lives back on track, and you went and took a great, steaming dump all over it!'

Travis sits forward suddenly, 'I didn't know!'

'That's because you're an idiot!'

'You said go get a loan and that's what I did!' Travis shoots back, getting annoyed. This was not all his fault, 'How was I supposed to know you already owed him money! You never told me!'

'You should have run it past me first!'

'You told me to sort it myself,' Travis goes on, 'Matt,

you said that you'd sort the van and pitch, if I sorted out the capital. You should have told me, 'Get some cash but whatever you do, don't go to fucking Baxter for it, I already owe him a grand!'

'I told you I needed to get out of a debt, Trav; that's what the van business was for!'

Travis stands, leaning over the table, jabbing his finger at Matt, 'You didn't say who!'

Cut Lip, Travis's escort, puts a hand on his shoulder, 'Bro, stop yelling at the cripple; it's not cool.' There is amusement in his tone, and he looks at the other man for smirking validation.

Travis allows himself to be sat again and Cut Lip steps back, muttering, 'You sound like a right pair of whiny bitches. Chill out a bit, yeah? I mean, I thought you were mates? Don't fall out over a burger-van.'

He thinks he's being funny. The other seems to think he is. Travis looks at Matt, at the tears that have appeared in the corner of his eyes. He wipes them quickly.

Travis closes his eyes, 'I still have time. Baxter gave me 3 days. I still have an hour and bit.'

Matt shakes his head. The anger has gone, just sadness remains, 'Where are you going to raise £10,000 in an hour?'

'I don't know, Matt,' Travis replies, his tone softened,

'But what else am I going to do? Sit here and have a pint with you?'

Matt stifled a chuckle, 'Think you might as well.'

A determined look crosses Travis's face, 'No, I want to see my son. I want to raise my son, Matt, that means *everything* to me. I'll get the money, if not tonight, even if I have - ' He looks at his healthy thighs, ' - that - I'll do it somehow even then.'

Travis stops. Matt is shaking his head.

'Fuck, you don't get it, Travis. Baxter's getting impatient about this whole thing. He sent me here as an encouragement because he wants it wrapped up as efficiently as possible. He doesn't want to hurt me or you; he wants his money. That is the best, most easy scenario for him. You *do* have until midnight, he says, but not a minute more because he's already given you a pass.'

Matt points at Travis's hand, 'If he doesn't get his money back, we're both on Strike Three.'

Travis's head starts to pound, as if his heart and his brain have swapped places, 'What – What - ?'

'What is Strike Three, Trav?'

Matt, his voice breaking and tears springing to his eyes again, points his finger straight, like a gun – or a drill. He lifts it from his thigh and presses his fingertip to his temple.

The white Range Rover bounces over the speed bump and pulls into the pub's car park. Bright white headlights flash across the width of the river, split by the metal rails. A man stands just the other side, an umbrella held over his head, turning as the illumination passes over him.

Cassandra pulls in, the large car neatly and purposely straddling two bays. The man ahead lifts an arm and waves with his free hand. She gives a little wave back and pushes the door open.

Her own umbrella flexes and expands into the rainy night as her heels hit the tarmac. She crosses the wet grass carefully, and clatters onto the paving stones.

The wide darkness of the River Trent sits before her at the bottom of the deep steps, a man-made bank. The water snakes away to her right, under the white suspension bridge towards Trent Bridge, with its constant stream of traffic hissing across it.

Ian stands by the edge of the concrete bank, watching her approach. 'I had a feeling that you'd call me, Cassandra.'

'And it is precisely that level of intuition that makes me trust you, Ian,' Cassandra replies, stopping by him.

Ian looks at her, 'I wish your husband did.'

'Michael's a fool, Ian,' Cassandra says, staring out at the south bank, and the brightly lit council building there, 'He didn't used to be, but um...'

'He's lost his edge in recent years.'

Cassandra nods, 'Yes. That's it. It would have been the loss of the Showroom, I think. He's not used to losing. It knocked him and he never recovered, although he thought he did.'

Ian sighs, 'I agree. It's a shame. It really is.'

A sudden breeze picks water up from the concrete ground, spatters them both with it along with the rain. Cassandra shakes off the chill, 'You need to make sure this deal goes through. There's a lot riding on it.'

'Believe me, Cassandra, I know,' Ian says, 'but Michael is not making it easy. He wants to make them sweat; says *he'll* make the call to accept the offer himself.'

Cassandra narrows her eyes, 'Do you think he will?'

Ian averts his eyes, searching for truth in the inky blackness of the Trent. Hundreds of years of history lay at the bottom of it, truths and lies, most forgotten, plenty more never known. 'I think he means to, yes.'

'That's not really an answer, Ian.'

'It's the most honest one I can provide.'

Cassandra inhales deeply, thinking before saying, 'You

know the other reason I trust you? Why I believe what you're telling is the truth? You're not trying to get into my pants.'

Ian grins and allows a little laugh, 'Yes, that's true.'

'Does Michael *know*?'

'I don't think he cares enough to care,' Ian says. 'I nod along with him when he's ogling some young waitress with too few buttons on her blouse, but he never asks about my personal life.'

'He's never met Tom?'

'In passing. You know what he's like. Anyone who is of no *use* to him is just white noise.'

Cassandra's expression fades into one of recollection, a memory of numerous years when Michael had simply looked through her. That was until he wanted something from her, and that something was only ever her body and what it could do for him. Half a decade she had devoted to him, taken the scraps of interest from him, readily accepted tiny morsels of affection with joy and elation. Given herself to him whenever he wanted because she did not know when her next validating meal would come.

He would discard her as soon as he was satisfied. She would retreat to the periphery of his life until required again. In time, she had begun to understand her place in his life, but, hanging onto the coattails of his meteoric rise in industry, feared to say anything in case he cast her aside.

It had been years before she grew both in self-confidence and understanding of the weapon she had always had and barely used.

The start of Michael's failures had come at the right time. She took control of their sexual agenda, denied more than she granted and took pleasure at his frustration.

Michael had always visited prostitutes. It was part of their dynamic, but he was foolish enough to believe in her ignorance of it. At first, she was scared to rock the boat; thereafter, she realised that his visits to them were not about sex.

They were about something else. And this was the root of Cassandra's new found power.

'Is the money I want secure?' she asks, looking directly at him.

Ian nods, 'As soon as the deal is agreed, the buyers will transfer the money through straight away. I've already spoken to Michael about investing a chunk offshore. He doesn't know that eighty grand is earmarked for you and your – investment.'

Ian stops. Cassandra raises an eyebrow, 'Problem?'

A Kiss At Midnight

'If you trust me, why won't you talk to me about this investment of yours?'

Cassandra turns and glances down the river, under the bridge. The football ground sits beyond, a beacon of perpetually fluctuating business and fan support.

'If Michael keeps his word, and gives me the money himself, I won't need it, Ian,' she tells him, 'It is the most important investment I will ever make, and you are my security. And to that end, promise me that if he doesn't call and finalize the deal – that you *will*. Please, don't lose it.'

Ian reaches out and touches Cassandra's arm, 'You have my word.'

9

Michael had sat and watched as Travis was ejected from the bar with the daft name. *A Bar Called Cafe. Seriously? That would be the first thing to go.*

Rain hammering on the windscreen, swept away by the wipers, he could see as the young man was shoved out into the squall, and with a forlorn look on his face, drifted off down the street.

Michael takes a long drink from a hip flask, then stows it back in the glove box. He opens the door and steps out into the wet, hurrying to the cover of the bar's door. The bouncers give him a cursory glance and allow him swift access to the dry warmth within.

Michael shakes the moisture from his hair and scans the

deep room. Still heaving with people, bassy music pounds in his ears and the smell of alcohol and body odour fills his nose. He heads towards the bar and over the heads can see staff moving; a tall, slim blonde with vulpine features and a large, stocky man who happens to look his way at the right moment. He smiles upon seeing Michael, and waves him over.

As bidden, Michael weaves his way to the end of the bar to find Sam already there, his huge hand thrust out to take Michael's.

'Michael, good to see you, darling,' Sam gushes, 'What brings you by?'

Michael shakes Sam's hand as firmly as he can, 'I was in the area, just thought I'd pop in to say hello to Camilla. Is she about?'

Sam makes a face and shakes his head, 'Yeah, she's about. Upstairs, I think.'

'Something wrong?' Michael asks with concern.

Sam throws his arms up in a grand gesture, 'Who the hell knows with her these days, Mike? I honestly don't know what her problem is.'

Michael replies, 'Have you told her?'

'Only that I'm selling the place. Thought it only fair, you know; she's been here forever. It's her home. I wanted to give her a fair warning,' Sam says, then sees

Michael's altered expression. 'I mean, if you're still interested. I haven't mentioned to her that it's *you* buying the place- '

Michael puts his hand on Sam's shoulder, 'Sam, it's fine.'

'You *are* still interested?'

Michael scoffs, throws his hand out to motion at the crowded room, 'Are you joking? Look at how busy this place is! Of course I want it!'

Sam grins broadly, 'Good! Great. We should get together, discuss things properly.'

'Of course, I'd like that,' Michael nods along, 'Next week, or week after. I'm sorry, I'll look at my diary properly tomorrow and give you a call.'

'Fine. No rush.'

'She's upstairs, you say? May I?'

Sam holds his arm up as an invitation towards the far door, 'Of course. And please, just remind her just how busy we are down here. I need her back behind this bar, soon as.'

Michael winks affirmation and shakes Sam's hand again before heading away, pushing his way back through the bar to the door. He pushes it open and starts to climb the steep, narrow stairs to the landing. There he looks at both doors, one ahead and one to the right; the latter being Camilla's flat. The other leads to the upstairs area, the top floor. Apparently, it is in need of serious refurbishment due to smoke damage from a minor incident years before Sam even took the place over. Michael will want to see it before he signs anything.

He tries the door; locked, as expected. No matter, one thing at a time.

Michael checks his watch. 10.27pm. He'll give it another forty-five minutes, then make the call to accept the offer. That'll satisfy him, keeping them hanging on, waiting, wondering. Then he'll tick Item 2 off his list, and in the meantime -

He gives the door a light, rhythmic tap and listens. Nothing at first, then a sudden movement of furniture; a chair or small table, then the scurrying of shoes across the wood floor.

The door is pulled open and Camilla's face appears, brow furrowed ready to deliver both barrels of verbal resentment, but upon seeing Michael, confusion sweeps across it.

'Um, hi,' she stutters, the confusion in turn changing to delight, 'Michael, what are you doing here? I thought Cassandra was coming later to pick up -'

Michael smiles warmly, leans on the door frame and holds up a hand to stop her, 'Relax, I'm not here for that. Whatever you arranged with Cassandra is still as it stood.

I was just in the area on business, thought I'd pop in, say hello... so, hello.'

He laughs at himself confidently, leading her to follow suit. She has a surprisingly girlish laugh for someone who seems to wear such a naturally serious expression; he likes it, and his own expression tells her that he does.

Despite herself, she looks away self-consciously. Only for a moment, but it gives Michael the opportunity to study her. She is so much shorter than Cassandra, her shape all different; where his wife is straight up and down, this girl is curvy. Cassandra is a clone of the glossy magazines she reads, whereas Camilla is entirely her own creation; new, exotic and undiscovered.

And, beyond all else, Cassandra has made it abundantly clear to him that sexual gratification will be given when she, and only she, decides.

She.

Who the hell does she think she is?

Michael is not controlled by anyone.

It is he who controls.

Camilla's head turns back and Michael realigns his gaze with hers. She cocks her head, shifting her dark hair subconsciously away from her face, 'Would you like to come in? I can put the kettle on.'

Michael smiles, 'I would love that.'

A Kiss At Midnight

*

Camilla hates that her heart flutters a little when she allows him past her. Her first memory of meeting him was his aftershave, and although she still has no clue as to what it is, she cannot help but think of him when she smells it somewhere.

She watches him walk into the middle of the room until he turns and smiles at her; another flutter and a swift self-admonishment. Camilla steps past him, heading to the kitchenette. She picks up the kettle, swills it to check the water level, and then clumsily fills it with water.

As she does, he pulls out one of the bar stools and sits at the counter that splits the living from the cooking area, slipping off his big coat and draping it across the worktop.

As Camilla drops the kettle back into its cradle, Michael speaks to her back, 'How's the little one?'

She turns, leans on the counter, hands behind her back, 'He's fine, yeah. Sleeping.'

'Sleeping through yet?'

'Not really. Wakes for a feed twice in the night, but settles right back down again.'

'Wow, good baby. I hear that's rare.'

'Yeah, again – so I hear too.'

They laugh together and Camilla takes two cups from the ornate metal mug tree, 'Did you want tea? Or coffee?'

Michael replies, 'Tea, please. Milk and none.'

Camilla nods, busies herself dropping tea bags into the cups and then stops, 'I'm sorry, I... I don't know how to be... it's weird.'

Michael exhales noisily, 'I understand, but it doesn't need to be weird, Camilla. It's just business.'

She turns, 'I know. I keep telling myself that, but even so -'

Michael holds up his hand, 'Are you sure you still want to do this?'

Camilla stops dumping sugar into her cup, looks right back at him, 'Totally. Michael, I totally want this.'

'I ask, because, I don't want Cassandra to get her hopes up and -'

'No! I want this, honestly,' Camilla states sharply, 'I need this - '

'Because if it's about money, there are other - '

Camilla steps towards him, teaspoon in hand, 'Michael... it's not about money. I mean, the money helps, for sure but... it's more than the money.'

A moment of silence passes between them, Michael staring at her, waiting.

God, she does like this about him; he listens. Actually listens to her. Most men she has known would jump in with words of advice, a declaration of what she should do or how she should feel; a farcical shining knight when all she wants is to be heard, not saved.

Camilla drops her elbows to the counter-top. She notices Michael's eyes flash to her cleavage for a fraction of a second, but does not mind too much. He's a nice guy, but he's still a guy. Attractive for a fifty year old, and she's always had a thing for blondes, and a good cologne, but that is where her interest firmly stops. In his prime, maybe; away from this whole baby-sale scenario, quite likely. But now... No chance; however, it's still nice to be found attractive by a sophisticated older man. A simple ego boost, nothing more.

'I've seen so many of my friends have babies who shouldn't have,' Camilla says, twirling the teaspoon in her fingers thoughtfully, 'And although they deny it, there is always that resentment there, at least at first. A wish that they hadn't. I've seen it, had them dance around conversations about how they feel about having it. Sure, at some point they convince themselves that they are doing the right thing by having the kid; be it during pregnancy, or in labour or when they celebrate its first birthday.

'But that's just it, Michael; they convince themselves. Either, I don't know, biological instinct kicks in, overriding their true feelings, or they talk themselves into it based on something... moral. In any case, they will, at some point regret it.'

Camilla looks at Michael, wondering if he's understanding her; if she's making sense. His gaze is steady, gives nothing away, but somehow invites more. She says, 'I don't hate kids. I don't, believe it or not, but do you know what they are, really?'

Michael shakes his head and Camilla answers, 'A tether. They tie you to the person you've had that kid with, and the best you can hope for is that you don't hate, or grow to hate, that person. Because from the point that baby is conceived, you are tied to that person *forever*. Even when that kid is grown up and having kids of their own, that other person will *always* be in your life.'

She suddenly pushes herself up, away back to the other counter, to where the kettle has clicked off. Steaming water gushes into the two cups, the inflated teabags floating on the surface, 'I can't be tethered to Travis for the rest of my life, Michael. I can't... I can't.'

She mutters as she yanks open the fridge, dumps milk into the cup, 'Did you say one?'

Michael frowns, 'Um, no, none.'

'Sorry,' Camilla mumbles and scoops two large servings of sugar into one cup, stirs both, and delivers one each to the counter and Michael's outstretched hands.

He sips it, smiles and makes the required 'ah' sound before asking, 'Is Travis so bad?'

Leaning again on the counter, Camilla inhales as she thinks, 'Strictly speaking, he's not a bad guy, in fact he's a lovely guy, or can be...but he is... toxic.'

'Toxic, okay.'

Camilla shakes her head, 'I know that sounds horrible, but he gets himself into things that he can't get out of, not without dragging someone else down with him. And for the three years we were together, that person was me.'

She sips her tea, and looks at Michael, 'Kicking him out was the best thing I ever did for myself. Problem was, it was after we, uh, fucked, one last time and...' A twirling hand describes the subsequent will of the Fates.

After a moment, Michael asks, 'If I may ask, Camilla... why did you not... terminate?'

'Because I was one of those idiots who convinced herself that having our baby was the right thing to do; that I didn't want or need Travis in our lives, that I could keep him out,' Camilla rattles on, aware that this was only half of the truth, but the purer half, 'But when I had my baby, and I looked into his little face, do you know what

A Kiss At Midnight

I saw?'

Michael replies, 'No?'

Camilla spits the name, 'Travis.'

10

After the two men had wheeled Matt away from the table and out of the pub, Travis had been unable to do anything but sit. Before leaving, they had placed a pint of Coors Light and bourbon chaser before him. He is sure it is some kind of joke, though it is beyond him.

Travis watches the bubbles form in the bottom of the glass, then rise through the amber liquid to join and become one with the foam at the top. Once that bubble pops into existence, its fate is inexorable. Physics, plain and simple, will steer it. It has no choice, no alternative. Events have been set in motion. There is no escape.

Travis snatches up the small shot of bourbon, tosses it back and regrets it immediately. His stomach tightens and Travis takes up the lager quickly, chugging it back.

Spirits had never agreed with him. In his teens, he had watched his friends with envy, as they pretended to enjoy a good, cheap scotch, or threw back shots of vodka or gallons of JD and coke. Confined to lagers or bitters, he found that by the time he was drunk enough on them to match his friends, his stomach had ballooned up with gas and his bladder was working overtime. Occasionally he succumbed to peer pressure, did a flavoured-shot, but every time he was redistributing it across the pavement half an hour later.

The lager does seem to settle his stomach and Travis leaves the table, dragging himself out of the pub, back into the rain and the night.

He wanders aimlessly, his mind see-sawing painfully between resolution to find some new plan, and resignation to a painful, inescapable death. Hard and unlikely, or an easy but tormented end. In the first option, he at least has a chance of seeing his son, despite Camilla making it clear that he couldn't if he did this. If he finds the money somehow, gets Baxter off his back, and proves to Camilla that his history of fucking things up is just that, surely she will come round.

What could he do? What *would* he do?

He stops, having wandered without taking note of

where he was going until he had noticed that the buildings had risen up either side of him, tall, closer than they usually were in Nottingham. He glances up. A short, covered bridge spans the gap between the two sides, four stories up.

Hounds Gate. He had walked in a loop, and if he carries on, he'll end up back at A Bar Called Cafe. Is his subconscious steering him back to Camilla, and his son?

Travis stops and leans back, looking skyward, searching for answers. Even if he does go back to her, he can't go back with nothing. Maybe he should just call it a day. Not go to Camilla, not wait for Baxter and his drill, deal with it himself.

Take his own life.

Travis scoffs to himself, loudly. Kill himself. As if. If he is honest with himself, he is too much of a coward to even give it serious consideration. He might entertain the idea for a while, but when it came down to the wire, he'd never go through with it.

He'd been to that dark place once before, not long before he had met Camilla. Despair and regret can do a lot, but they can't make you grow a pair of balls.

A deep honk snaps him out of his reverie, and instinctively, he leaps to the side. A car revs past him, the driver not looking at him but shaking his head. It drives on a few yards and then pulls into a little lay-by on the left, stopping.

It is a silver Volkswagen Passat, the previous year's model, a typical mid-range corporate car. The sort of thing that Travis used to think he'd end up driving one day, once he'd started his business and its success had sucked him into a bright future. That guy had money; not a huge amount, but sufficient to live well enough.

An idea forms in his mind, a plan almost as scary as killing himself.

The door opens and a man steps out, umbrella first; a suit under a big coat, portly, though not fat and a balding head rimmed with dark hair. He yammers into a phone as he fumbles a briefcase out after him.

'I know what I said, Tom, but I told you that tonight would be a late one,' he says, 'Alright, I said complicated, but it amounts to the same thing… I don't know, couple of hours, I imagine… just go to bed, I'll be in when I'm in… fair enough, fine… I love you, night.'

The man starts dialling another number and slams the door shut.

Travis is already moving. Travelling forward without any idea what he's going to do when he reaches his destination. His footsteps are hidden by the rain until he is only a few feet away.

The man is starting to walk away, orange lights blinking briefly behind him, when he seems to sense something and turns.

It is that turn that jolts Travis into decision, into action. Still, no plan, he acts without thought, lifting his guitar case and swinging it.

The impact causes the man's head to swivel, its own momentum dragging the body after it. Blood gushes from his nose, his feet tip onto their edges. Hands reach out, grasping at air.

Adrenaline pumping, Travis swings the guitar case again and this time hits the man in the chest as he spins. The phone flies out of his hand as he tumbles against the car; it drops to the ground and he seems to cry out to it.

Travis moves in, lifts a fist and strikes.

His hands are small, his fists unused to fighting, his experience limited to sofa-wrestling his younger brother. His knuckles bounce off the back of the man's head and pain shoots up the tendons on his hand.

The man turns, face pouring red, grabs at Travis's collar and pushes him back, but his intent is not to fight back, but to get to the phone on the floor. Travis pushes back, his right leg shooting backwards for leverage.

There is a crack of glass and plastic, and the man cries out, his face contorting with anger. He is significantly stronger than Travis, and twists his wrists, pulling Travis away before rolling his chubby fingers into a ball and driving it into his assailant's cheek.

Lights flash in Travis's vision and he stumbles. The scream of the drill rips through his mind and for a second, he is not sure where he is. He feels that he is being pushed and jerks.

The man is swung around, and in turn swings Travis until their combined momentum is beyond either of their control. It is Travis who trips over his own feet and dives, but the portly man's greater weight keeps Travis aloft, but sends them both, at speed, into a black, concrete bollard.

*

Michael is enjoying himself. Now seated in the living area on the cheap white leather sofa, his tea cooling in his hands, Camilla is still talking about her relationship with Travis. Nodding along, ensuring his eyes meet hers when she looks up, it appears that he is hanging on her every word.

In truth, he remembers, at best, every other word. Michael feels that one of his best skills is appearing to be fully engaged in a conversation, whilst allowing his mind to wander off, and yet pick up on important things in order to perpetuate the dialogue. Conversely, he can also appear entirely bored, yet track the conversation precisely. Both techniques have proven useful over the years, both in business dealings, and in those of a more personal nature.

It comes down to control of the situation. Decide on the most desirable outcome, plan your moves, plan *their* moves, and be patient in seeing it through.

Michael has been going through the method since the door was opened to him. He has long since decided its outcome.

If Cassandra is going to get what she wants from this young woman, then so is he.

Camilla's rattling monologue comes to a natural end and Michael jumps in before she can start another chapter, 'Well. I'm sure Sam won't see you homeless, Camilla.'

She snorts impudently, 'I don't know any more, Michael. I thought I knew him. I thought he was more than my boss and my landlord, I thought he was my friend.'

Michael smiles as though he understands. What he does understand, however, is how childish and small-minded she is. Sam is clearly doing the best he can by her, but when push comes to shove, he is not beholden to her; Camilla is not actually his daughter. He has his own life, and Michael is making Sam a very decent offer.

Such a silly girl. She has no foresight.

He studies her face. Her mouth is pinched angrily; her brow furrowed, she mutters under her breath, 'He's such a dickhead.'

Michael smiles; *time for another move.*

He slides towards her, places his mug down on the wood floor and uses that hand to press hers. Surprised at the contact, she looks up at him, but doesn't recoil.

Good.

Michael exhales slowly before he speaks, 'I know that you're angry at Sam, but sometimes there are more things moving than you can see.'

'What do you mean?'

'What do you know about the person he's selling to?'

Camilla shakes her head, 'Nothing. The twat won't tell me anything.'

Michael squeezes her hand and says, 'I feel your frustration, Camilla. I do. And I understand why you're selling your baby to Cassandra – '

'And you,' Camilla chips in quickly, smiling, 'To both of you.'

Michael half-nods, 'Of course, to both of us.' He

coughs, realigns the conversation, 'I understand why. I know what you've lost; your feeling of being *chained* to someone you dislike. You feel alone, isolated... you just want *your life* back.'

He watches Camilla's throat undulate, her eyes flicker, glisten, and squeezes her hand a little tighter, 'You deserve to have your life back. None of this is your fault.'

Her mouth opens to reply, but her throat is full of emotion. She nods and shakes her head all at once.

Score. Direct hit to a raw nerve.

Camilla voice is low as she speaks, 'I just want to live again, Michael - '

He moves his hand, lifts his arms to embrace her, pulls her face into his shoulder, and feels her expel a single sob. A hand rests gently against the back of her head, stroking her hair. The other drops to her lower back. She doesn't move away. He feels her relax into him.

Time to step things up.

'What if I told you that you had nothing to worry about. That you didn't have to move. That after your deal with Cassandra was done, you could stay here for as long as you liked?' Michael says slowly, ensuring that every word is understood, 'And that you would never have to worry about money again, either?'

'What?' Camilla whispers, pulling away enough to look

up into his eyes, 'How could..?'

Michael goes for broke, uses the back of a finger to stroke her cheek, 'I'm the buyer.'

11

The thud rattles Travis as, still moving, he sprawls across the wet tarmac.

On his front, soaked to the skin, Travis brushes his sopping hair away from his eyes to see the man lying on his side. He is moaning, but doesn't move much, only his feet scraping along the ground, back and forth.

Travis looks around. There is no one in the immediate vicinity. A group walking further up, by Maid Marian Way; other voices echoing somewhere.

Breathing hard, he scrambles back to the man, who is groaning, his eyes rolling around. They lock on Travis as he appears over him and he tries to reach out, either to grab or block him. One hand grabs for Travis's face, but the other hangs limply on the ground at an awkward angle.

Travis grabs the wrist of the reaching arm, flings it away. The sharp movement makes the man cry out and clutch his other shoulder. Looking down where his coat is falling away, blood is seeping through his white shirt, something else poking up into the fabric, threatening to split it.

The man moans and Travis looks about again. Still alone. Still time. He's come this far.

Travis pulls at the man's coat, who still tries to fight back, but the pain in his neck and shoulder prohibit any effective counter measures. Yanking the coat, thrusting his hands into the outside pockets, Travis finds only a handkerchief and a Lion bar wrapper; in the other, a set of earphones.

Travis tears the coat open, sending buttons spinning across the tarmac and pulls the contents of the inside pockets out. There is something large and flat there.

He removes it quickly. A wallet.

The man groans again, reaches out for it, tries to snatch it back.

Finally, Travis loses what little nerve he has and stands, wallet in hand, backing away. As he grabs his guitar case and scuttles away up the street, the man continues to lie on the wet ground, his one good arm clutching at its shattered twin.

For the first time in a long time, Travis is optimistic. The wallet in his hand feels full, bulging out. Travis reaches the top of the street, where Castle Gate meets Maid Marion Way at a T, wide and open. To his right is the Royal Children, an historic pub busy with regulars. As he stands there, a small group are exiting, cigarettes in hand, looking ruefully at the rain.

Travis suddenly feels exposed. He glances back at the man, but cannot see him in the gloom, or even hear him now. Turning away from the light of the pub, he crosses Castle Gate and walks parallel with Maid Marion Way for a few yards.

On his left, St. Nicholas Church looms over him, a dark yard guarding it. He hops up the low wall and heads across the saturated grass, towards the rear of the old building. There, a small recess sits, cloaked in darkness away from street lamps.

He dives into it, pressing himself against the wall, comforted by the shadow around him. He tries to calm his breathing, slow his heart, but his mind is consumed by the act of violence he has just committed.

And of course it comes, unwanted but expected.

Vomit ploughs up his gullet, explodes from his mouth

and across the dark walls. He coughs and retches again, but nothing more comes. His stomach tightens. He drops to his knees.

That poor guy. He didn't deserve that. But Travis was desperate. It was just money, and that guy clearly had enough.

The wallet. Travis pulls out his phone, flicks on the torch and grips it in his teeth. He opens the bulging wallet out, sees the wedge of paper inside and excitedly pulls it out.

A thick pile of twenty pound notes.

Thank fuck.

His hand shaking, he counts it, and as he does, his excitement fades into cold realisation of both the violence he has committed, and the futility of it.

The final count, £465. Travis clutches the money in his hand and lets out a wail, banging the back of his head against the wall.

On a normal day, to have that amount of cash in his hands would be a blessing, but in this moment, it was a joke at his expense. It was not even a fraction of what he owed to Baxter.

*

A Kiss At Midnight

Michael waits patiently for Camilla to reply. Watches her eyes as the information sinks in, processing, making sense of it, deciding how to react. She is clearly hot-headed, a passionate woman whose mouth is often running away long before her brain has even had chance to consider anything, but now she is taking her time. Her mouth is open, ready to speak, but her lips have pursed slightly, a barely restrained sign of anger. Gears turn behind her green eyes, assessing and calculating.

It amuses him, but he keeps his expression earnest. What an interesting young woman, so naïve yet self-assured, her confidence and clumsy beauty off-setting the truth of her pathetic ingenuousness.

He will enjoy her.

It was a slice of pure luck that he met her those few months ago. Pure chance had seen him meeting prospective investors in A Bar Called Cafe, a meeting that had gone so poorly that upon their leaving, Michael had started to question himself and his ability. Such self-sorrow was short lived, however, when the bar's owner, Sam, fell into conversation with him. Sam too was in a state of crisis, questioning whether he was on the right path in life; if running this place was what he wanted to do, or if he was doing it simply because it was what he knew. It was the safe option. In his heart, he confessed that he truly wanted to sell.

And Michael, knowing that he sorely needed a financial lifeline, was interested in buying something like it.

The drinks had flowed, resulting in a hasty agreement to discuss a possible deal further as soon as they were sober. In truth, both men were desperate to appear to be the shrewd businessmen they felt they were, and although feigned cautiousness, were more worried about the other party backing out.

Sure enough, a week later, a deal had been made to follow through on the sale within the next couple of months. It was during Michael's visits to the bar, to ascertain its viability, but also to escape Cassandra, who had recently begun to voice her obsession to have a baby, and withhold sex until he granted it. It was at the height of his frustration at this impossible situation that he met one of Sam's barmaids, exotic and oddly attractive despite her swollen abdomen.

Camilla worked little during this time, waddling about during quieter periods, supporting her stomach with one hand and carrying a fist-full of empty glasses with the other. Michael, who had always taken pride in making a show of chivalry, had, when she appeared to be really struggling, insisted on taking a heavy tray from her.

A Kiss At Midnight

At first, she seemed displeased by his help, but he had won her round with his usual, heavy-handed charm offensive, whereupon she gave him a few drinks on the house. Camilla, not planning on winning any mother of year awards, joined him and together they descended into a jovial and comfortable state of inebriation.

It was here that she let slip her misery at having her baby, confessed that she wished that she wasn't. A spark flickered into creation, deep into Michael's mind. A burst of light that grew, spreading outward, formless at first, before growing, evolving, becoming an idea that would define everything he would do for the next few months.

Michael would revive his ailing career. Cassandra would have her damned baby, and would submit to him once again. Yet, beyond this, such was his anger at Cassandra tonight for denying him *her*, he would take something else. An additional purchase. Another investment.

Camilla speaks finally, and pulls herself away from Michael as she does, 'Are you fucking serious?'

Michael sighs with gratification, silently, inwardly and lets her pull away from him, leads her with, 'Camilla - '

'No!' she stands up angrily, steps away, 'You lied to me! I thought you were a friend... you fucking prick!'

Michael watches as she unleashes a tirade of abuse, a

badly thought out, grammatically shameful, verbal assault, swirling around her main point in a dizzying cycle of fury and hurt. Her mind is left far behind and her mouth runs on and on until it cannot find any further combinations of her finite source of expletives.

Camilla, breathless, stops and turns to the side window, leaning on the chair. She stares at the dried-up Christmas tree, silent and lost in her thoughts.

Another move.

Michael stands and crosses to her, puts his hands on her shoulder. Immediately, she shakes them off and he allows it, saying quietly, 'Camilla... I want you to stay. I never meant to hurt you, but I was worried about telling you.'

The back of her head is expressionless. He continues, 'I know we don't know each other that well, but I thought you might react... like this.'

She turns sharply, looks up at him challengingly, 'Like this? You mean pissed off because another dick-head man is trying to ruin my life?'

Michael puts his hands on her arms, squeezing them. She doesn't flinch at the touch, 'I'm not trying to ruin your life, Camilla. I promise, I'm trying to help you get it back.'

She looks up at him. The anger is still there, but it has

ceased to bubble and swirl. Michael continues, 'I want you to take your life back. Back to before. To when it was yours. Before Travis, before the baby. To when you were *you*.'

Then he sees it. The anger is evaporated. The V between her brows lifts away. Her eyes soften.

Penultimate move. Make the offer, take it away. Make them fear its loss. Make them *want* it.

Michael shakes his head, his tone has changed, now sorrowful, 'I'm so sorry, I've over-stepped. Forget I said anything.'

Suddenly and sharply, he turns away from her.

12

The cars pass beneath. A river of metal and rubber, rushing and swirling, mixing and gushing onwards to a delta that will never exist.

Travis pictures himself falling. Fifty feet will take only a few seconds, but given the intensity of the traffic, it will be seconds more before he reaches the ground. He'll most likely hit a bus first; his spine will crack the window of the top deck, bounce him away, spin him like a Catherine wheel onto the hard bonnet of another car. He'll be carried by the current of inertia, flung off by the sudden braking and his face will implode against the loading gate of a pickup up truck.

His body will be broken, but will it be enough? Will he

lie there, unable to move? Will his lungs and his heart and his mind fight to keep him alive, in pain, but breathing, thinking, feeling?

What if he dives off? Goes head first? He is no athlete, has no core strength. If his body flips, he can do nothing to correct it. He'll land on his back, and then all he can hope for is that a family SUV will react too slowly and crush his skull with its oversized tyres.

What if it doesn't?

Travis looks away from the cars racing away beneath him, feels the rain lashing his face. Standing on the Arndale car park, on a section of the multi-storey that spans Maid Marion Way, he feels powerless.

He has tried everything, and everything has failed. To make money, to create a life for himself. To meet his son, his own flesh and blood, even that has been denied. Even his life, and the means to end it is closed to him, barricaded by his own cowardly over-thinking.

Is he crying? His chest heaves, his throat tight but the rain hides any tears. The roar of the traffic drowns out his sobs. The patter of the rain on his coat, the honking of impatience from below, the melody of a phone.

He looks down, so suddenly, he makes himself dizzy.

A phone is ringing.

He snatches his mobile out of his pocket; the screen is

dark, but he can hear it ringing. Perhaps the screen was damaged in the fight.

Travis presses the green button and puts it to his ear, 'Cammy?'

No answer. Silence. Not even static.

But the ringing continues. A stupid polyphonic orchestra.

Travis frowns, stares at his mobile. That is not his ring tone.

He pats his pockets, finds a lump and pulls it out. It is the phone from the man he had attacked.

The broad smartphone screen is lit up and flashing a mobile number.

Unsure of what to do, Travis stares at it until it stops. Seconds later, it starts again.

Water running down his face in rivulets, Travis looks down at the cars below. Any one of them could be his executioner. Perhaps this caller could be his salvation.

Timidly, he presses the green icon on the screen, and a male voice barks at him.

'About time you answered you miserable fucking faggot! I told you when we spoke earlier that I was not someone to fuck about with. I want to speak with your boss now. Get him on the phone right this fucking second. I want this deal confirmed. I want that land and I want it signed off right fucking now, you prick. You listening? Ay, you there or - '

Travis hangs up. His chest is tight again, his head pounding. How on earth do these things happen to him every time? That could have been a wife calling to check in, a child at university ringing for a chat, a friend, a colleague, even a radio station informing a winner of ten grand.

No. This is Travis. Of course it is a furious and aggressive man.

Travis shakes his head. No more. He is done.

No more trying.

No more thinking.

He holds the man's smartphone over the side and drops it. Doesn't watch it topple into the darkness to be annihilated by the impact.

Travis steps up onto the slippery metal barriers beside the wall.

The tarmac river flows beneath him. It will drown him quickly. There will be no pain. Only darkness. Only peace. If only he could have seen his son, just once -

Without warning, the soft rubber of his trainers slips and he tips forward. His resolve is gone a moment before and he screams, reaching out for support that is not there.

His head goes over the edge, pulling his body. He is flying, and painfully aware that he is falling back first, straight down.

*

To when you were you.
The words are still echoing in Camilla's head when Michael suddenly turns from her.

She needs a moment, to process what he is saying. Stepping away to the kitchen, she turns and leans against the side. Her fingers grip the counter edge, finding a grip on the reality she suddenly faces. An anchor to the present.

Michael is standing, his head bowed like he is kicking himself. To his left, across the room in the Christmas tree, brittle and dry, the home-made ignition device lies hidden behind the chair.

Camilla runs the conversation through her head. It is jumbled. She tries to pick out bullet points, tries to order them, so that they make sense.

Travis is there, his miserable face staring helplessly over the bar at her.

Cassandra, her elegance and her aloof nature, her guard down only when she is staring into the face of the baby.

Michael's earnest face. Honest and compassionate, apparently willing to help her.

Camilla's long thought out plan, an idea born out of quiet desperation, all its elements carefully ordered.

One, Cassandra would pay her the hundred grand and take the baby away. The tether to Travis would be cut forever. She would be free of him.

Two, Camilla would burn down the flat and possibly the bar if the fire spread that far. A final *fuck you* to her 'friend' Sam, and more importantly, time bought, giving her time to get on a plane to where ever she wanted. By the time the rescue services realised there was in fact no one in the flat, she would be gone.

Three, she would start a new life. A hundred thousand pounds would get her started comfortably, tide her over while she bought a cheap apartment on a Mediterranean resort island, assumed a new name, got a bar job on a beach front. She would live the quiet, content life that she deserved. That she should have had.

Away from here.

Away from home.

The tree. She has never committed arson before. Never done more than stolen a packet of crisps from the newsagent, or a scarf from New Look. The police WOULD look for her, she knows this. She would spend the rest of her life looking over her shoulder, never able to fully relax, even in paradise.

Camilla looks again at Michael.

No baby. Keep her flat. Work for someone who cares for her.

Temptation begins to prod at her.

'I could keep living here?' Her voice is quiet, more timid than she wants it to be. She coughs, clearing her throat, 'Keep working here?'

Michael turns, looking her in the eye, 'For as long as you wanted to, Camilla. You'd be free again. Free to be yourself.'

Camilla furrows her brow and Michael turns fully to face her, 'I'm sorry I kept my buying the bar from you. I knew you'd be knocked around by life, taken for granted by people who said they cared for you.'

He steps closer, looks down at her, smiling, 'I just wanted to protect you.'

Camilla looks up at him and feels the dread of carrying out her plan starting to drain away. She always feared it, its potential repercussions. She is no fool, knowing the consequences of what she is doing, but feels that she has to be brave. To push through. To get to the other side. To her paradise. The truth is, this is her paradise. She has no grand plans. This flat, her job, this city is all she ever really wanted.

Her chin drops, her gaze unable to stay with his as the two paths threaten to pull her apart.

His hands fall to his arms and he steps in again, 'It is entirely *your* choice, Camilla. Choose what feels right to you.'

His left hand moves from her arm, to her waist and rests against the curve of her hip.

It is an unexpected weight. An uncomfortable weight.

One of the bullet points of the earlier conversation comes barrelling to the front of her mind.

'Why would I never have to worry about money again?'

Michael shrugs, runs his right hand down her arm, to her hand, squeezing it, 'Because I would look after you.'

Camilla smiles back at him, 'Why would I need looking after? If I have the money from the baby, and I keep the flat, and keep working at the bar, I'd be paying you rent easily.'

Michael replies softly, 'I wouldn't want you to pay rent. You'd be set. Nothing to pay.'

'There is always something to pay.'

Then is lips are on hers. A pressure against her mouth suddenly, his hot breath racing across her face.

The surprise of it freezes her. It is only when his hand slips further around her waist, to her back, pulling her closer, that she pushes him gently.

Palms against his chest, she presses, pulls her neck away, turns her head.

'Michael...' she says calmly. Camilla is not angry, flattered in his interested. There has been a misunderstanding somewhere, an innocent comment from her perhaps, misconstrued. She was comfortable with him, maybe he took it as flirting. She doesn't want to hurt his feelings. She wants her flat.

But his lips are on her cheek and her neck. She squirms, trying to slide out from under him, 'Michael, I'm sorry but...'

'You'll never want for anything,' he mutters between wet kisses. His left hand moves to her shoulder, his right to his neck, cradling her there.

You'll never want for anything.

The words suddenly chill her. Their true meaning.

She was right. *There is always something to pay.*

'No!' she cries out suddenly, using more force to push him away enough for her to slide out, 'I'm not interested in being your fucking whore!'

He grabs her waist, pulling her back. She turns, pushing him against the main counter, but he follows her into the corner of the other counter, pinning her, 'Get the fuck off me!'

Fury rises in her. Another man using her, harassing her, bullying her, steering her. Another person she trusted turning on her to satisfy their own will, their own designs and desires.

Rage fuelled, she reaches up to his face, grabs at him, nails digging in to his skin.

How dare he?!

Michael cries out, an inhuman bellow and grabs her hands, pulling them away from his face, 'Camilla, please... you've misunderstood - '

She spits at him. A bullet of mucus hitting him in the cheek, dribbling down across his open mouth. His face contorts, twisting into a mural of pure hatred. He tries to twist her wrists, but despite her smaller stature, Camilla has never been weak. She struggles against him, wriggling, trying to create a better position to push back.

The more she fights him, the more enraged he becomes. He jerks, she loses her gains and he twists her arms, stepping back.

Camilla tries to move, but he uses the extra space to turn her and push her against the counter. He grabs her hair, pulling it. His hand grabs at her waist band, yanking it so that the button on her jeans pops off.

Then his other hand is on her face, his breath hot in her ear. She can feel his fingers creeping across her cheek, towards her mouth.

His voice is so different now. No longer friendly, charming, confident; it is a growl, choler-filled and frustrated.

'Open your mouth.'

For the first time, genuine fear bites at Camilla. Gritting her teeth, she kicks out, trying to drive her foot into his knee or his crotch. He avoids it, starts pulling at her top and leans down to her ear again.

'Open it.'

Camilla lets out a little moan and shakes her head away, clamping her jaw shut, locking her lips as tight as she can, as the probing digit pushes between them.

A throaty growl from his throat. Fear of his sudden and unexpected intentions collide with a ball of white hot fury in Camilla, an ignition of sheer will as he goes on.

'Why do you women not understand that I am to be obeyed?', he hisses, 'I know what is best for you. I am not to be fucked with; you will learn this, and my wife will eventually learn - '

His own blood pouring down the back of his throat ends the mission statement, soaking the back of Camilla's head too.

Michael stumbles backwards a little bit, pain, fury, and indignation burning in his eyes as he clutches at the broken pulp of his nose.

But his rage is only a spark when compared to that of Camilla as she turns to face him, her hand on his throat. She lifts her knee and drives it between his legs, screaming out as she does.

Blood boiling, head spinning, control having long since left her, Camilla grabs the knife block from the side. It is filled with knives of all kinds, from bread to steak to peelers, but they all tip out as she lifts it.

Two hands are needed to raises it above her head, and even then, they strain. Steel rimmed, polished granite. It was a gift from her sister, a house-warming present, marked down from a catalogue shop.

Consequences.

They hit her when the solid knife block has begun its swift descent. About half way, Camilla suddenly realises what she is doing, but the time to alter her plans has long since passed.

The granite is too heavy to slow. Physics has taken control and refuses to yield.

It sounds more like a pop, rather than a crunch, and Michael's head snaps away disturbingly fast.

The weight and speed rips the block from Camilla's grasp and it flies across the kitchen, hitting the cupboard door and cracking it before falling to the linoleum floor.

Camilla falls away, trying to grab the counter, but she misses and sprawls on the carpeted living area.

She waits for Michael to move, to continue the fight. She was not going to run. This was her home.

Breathing hard, she waits.

After a moment, she kicks at Michael's feet, but gets no response. Not even a moan.

She kicks again, harder.

Still nothing.

Slowly, she rises to her knee, picks up one of the many knives scattered around her, and moves towards him on her knees.

As she draws closer, she can see his head turned away. There is blood on the floor under it, a crimson halo spreading slowly.

She stands, using the counter to pull herself up, and looks at his face.

A strangled gasp bursts from her mouth.

One of his eyes is closed, blood from his nose spattered across his eye lid. It is the other eye that bothers her.

At first, it appears wide open, but the extent of its bulging confuses her. Then understanding hits. The eye lid now sits behind the eyeball, and the brow above the socket is indented, cracked. There is no longer space for it inside the skull, so it has, in part, exited.

A Kiss At Midnight

Camilla turns away and vomits.

13

Death hurts. It feels like a bad massage. Stabs of pain throbbing along his back, shoulders feeling like they've been crushed and he's winded in a way he has never known.

Travis can't breathe. His lungs won't allow themselves to be inflated enough catch any air.

That is when he knows he is not dead.

Not breathing is a big part of death.

His ears are ringing, drops of water are filling his mouth and nose, air is rushing over him.

He opens his eyes and for a moment, it is dark. Shifting geometric shapes inches above him, then clear, dark sky and the rain again.

His hands reach out, like he's making a snow angel. His fingertips touch the ground; it is cold and metal.

Travis turns his head, looks to the side. The wall of Broadmarsh Centre is moving past.

He inhales, it hurts, but he can get more air. Another breath. His head clears.

There is a squeal and the world stops moving. A hiss, a clunk. There are people talking, shouting.

Travis turns onto his side, looks around; there are no doors on the walls, only windows, and signs. No cars around him.

Confusion finally gives way to awful clarity as he realizes he is lying on the roof of a double decker bus.

He inhales as fully as he can. It hurts like hell, his ribs crack and he sits up. There is still a ringing in his ears.

People are talking below. He can hear them discussing what the bang was, hypothesizing and theorizing.

Travis stays flat, understanding his bizarre and unexpected predicament. He rubs his head, pokes his ears trying to get rid of the ringing.

So loud, even the people on the ground are discussing the ringing -

Travis stops. It is a shrill sound, but rhythmic, pulsing.

He pats his pocket, and takes out the smartphone that rang before. Its screen is dark, the speaker silent.

In his other pocket, his own phone. Screen bright, screaming at him.

An unknown number.

Staying low, keeping his voice down, he answers though it hurts to talk, 'Hello?'

'Travis, thank god.'

'Cammy?'

A pause, then, 'Yeah, it's me – I – Travis, I need you.'

Travis frowns, suddenly less sure that he survived the fall from the multi-storey. That he didn't fuck it up. That this isn't in fact some version of heaven in which things do actually work out for him. Camilla *needs* him.

'What?' he asks, finding his voice.

Camilla's voice is odd, like she is crying, 'Something's happened, Travis. I need help. Please come back to the bar.'

Below, the voices are now discussing the police.

'Travis? Are you there?'

'I'm coming, Cammy,' Travis replies quickly, gathering his thoughts fully, 'I'll be in there in a few minutes.'

Camilla breathes heavily down the line, 'Thank you, I'll leave the back door open. You remember the back door?'

'Of course.'

'Okay.'

Then she is gone. Travis slides the phone back into his

pocket and crawls towards the edge of the bus by the street, away from the pavement and the people.

He glances back up at the car park, the part that spans the road where he fell. It must have been fifteen feet, between the top and the bus's roof.

Suddenly, he remembers. His guitar is there, propped against the concrete wall. Dammit. Nothing he can do, and anyway, he now has the opportunity to see his son. A good trade.

Smiling his first genuine smile in a long time, Travis looks over the edge. The road seems very far below, and cars are whizzing past, stopping only briefly, then speeding on.

Even dropping down feet first, he might break his ankle. How the hell can he get down at all, let alone not attract attention?

There, a transit van pulling up alongside. Onto that, then the remaining eight feet to the ground.

Decision made, but the van is already moving on. Panicked, Travis swings his legs over the side and jerks his body into the air, towards the van.

He hits the roof with his feet just as it starts to move, spilling him sideways. He turns, tries to grab onto the bus, falls backwards and slides brutally down the windows.

The ground hits him hard, but he is driven. He is on his feet and running, through the traffic, away from the shouts of the self-proclaimed detectives behind.

*

Camilla wonders if she's made a mistake.

Sitting on the white leather sofa, shoulders hunched, hands pressed together on her knees, her eyes are fixed on the inert hand on the faux tiled floor.

Its fingers are curled up, like a spider becoming dried and crispy on a windowsill in summer.

She had panicked. Things had gone from right, to better, to awful in the space of seconds. Camilla felt she was finally starting to regain control of things, and then this conniving, chauvinist bastard had tried to take the power away from her.

For a moment, in the heat of the struggle, she fought back, retook the high ground, only to lose it again.

She had called Travis.

She had regressed to a time when Travis was her rock, her confidant and her best friend; the one person she could turn to for everything. It had been natural. An instinct long buried, erupting, spewing out her inner weakness.

Camilla growls into her hands, bunching them into fists, and curses herself.

She looks at the hand. A little red river picks its way through the detail of the linoleum.

She could have dealt with that herself if she'd just given herself an extra moment to breathe. But no, she had grabbed that stupid ultrasound photo from the side and dialled Travis's mobile.

Another growl, which becomes a bellow and a demented cry.

Silence follows it.

Think.

Camilla stands up, sees the Christmas tree, set up, waiting. The clock reads 11.35.

Travis will be here any moment, Cassandra is on her way. Her husband is in her kitchen.

She frowns hard, trying to order her moves, when a succession of dull clangs echoes out from the back of the flat.

*

Cassandra glances at the clock just as it changes from 11.37 to 11.38, then rattles the plastic until the little nylon strap found its way through the narrow slit.

Surely this isn't right. It's too small, too tight. It's what the instructions say. It must be wrong.

She grunts as she strains and is about to give up when her manicured fingers find the other end and grip it tightly, pulling.

The strap finally feeds neatly through the back of the car seat, allowing her to loop it around the front, and finally reunites the seatbelt

Letting out a gasp of relief, Cassandra sits back on the other rear seat, looks down at her handiwork. A fine looking baby seat. It should be, it cost as much as she pays for shoes.

Only one thing missing now.

Smiling, she envisions the seat's little passenger, gurgling away and staring up at her with the love she deserves.

The clock on the Range Rover's dashboard flickers to 11.44.

She'll give it another few minutes to make sure she doesn't seem to eager. Let Camilla think that she might have changed her mind. Besides, truth be told, she feels far more comfortable going in there after Ian had called her confirming the property sale had all gone through fine.

Cassandra wasn't worried. Ian was a solid, reliable person, perhaps the only one she knew. He'd get it done, even Michael himself was proving an obstacle. And Ian would make sure Cassandra got the money she needed for the baby. Michael's mercurial nature would not ruin her own happiness this time.

Even if there was a blip, she had £10,000 pounds in cash in her purse. A physical demonstration she knew that silly girl upstairs would be impressed enough by to give her the benefit of the doubt in case the money transfer to her was late.

Cassandra leans over to the front passenger seat, grabs her purse and flicks on the interior light. In the dim light, she reapplies her lip gloss, using action as a mental distraction.

*

Water pours off the broken gutter above the thick metal door, creating a waterfall that splits when it clicks and is pushed open.

Travis, soaked to the bone, smiles broadly at Camilla. The door rattles as it hits the gantry, her hand remaining on the handle.

She stares back at him, her expression hidden in shadow by the strong yellow light behind her.

Travis opens his mouth to say something, perhaps thank you, or please don't change your mind now. Instead, Camilla steps forward suddenly, out into the rain and throws her arms around his neck.

In that second, everything melts away; his aching back, the mugging, Matt, Baxter, the money and the drill. He wraps his arms around her, buries his face in her hair and breathes her in.

He is home.

He loses track of how long they stand there, knows only that it is not nearly long enough.

Camilla peels herself away from him gently and looks up into his eyes, 'Come inside.'

She takes his hand and leads him inside, stopping only to pull the door shut, and leads him round the short corridor. He notices a bedroom door shut before they enter the flat's main room, and memories come flooding back to him. The white leather sofa he insisted on when Camilla wanted black, the television he bought without consulting her, the chair in the corner that he had brought from his childhood bedroom. A dried up Christmas tree now standing behind it. A flickering cine-film of moments playing back all at once; birthdays, Christmases, impromptu house parties and quiet dinners together, and all the places they had had sex.

Camilla sees him looking around and lets his hand go, stepping away before saying, 'I changed a few things.'

Travis nods, 'I can see. I like the picture.' It is a lake at sunset, a jetty projecting out into the water symmetrically.

Camilla smiles, still frowning, 'Travis, I'm sorry I was a bitch earlier. You just - '

'I surprised you,' Travis interjects, stepping forward, 'I just needed to see you, I didn't think things through. I know I never do, and I'm sorry, Cammy. So sorry for everything. Everything I ever done - '

It is Camilla who step towards him now, holding up her hand to stop him 'It's okay, Travis. That's... I guess that's all in the past now. It doesn't matter. There are other things we need to talk about. More important. More urgent.'

She closes the gap between them. Travis's heart leaps. She is as beautiful as he remembers, more so; more confident, more focused, but there is that old vulnerability radiating from her that always made him feel so needed. Something he had never had from anywhere else.

A Kiss At Midnight

He wants to kiss her and lets her take his hand, but instead she leads him from the corridor's mouth, around the kitchen counter and stops.

She waits for his eyes to drop to the floor.

14

Ian feels like he is drowning. He coughs and tries to turn his head, but the water seems to keep finding its way into his mouth. It's cold and tastes like car fumes.
Where is my phone?
He moves his left hand, searching the rough ground around him. When he finds nothing, he moves his right and cries out. It is pain like he has never known, shooting up his shoulder, into his chest, making him gasp.

He tries again, and cries out once more. Ian is not even sure if his hand is even moving.

Ian's vision is blurred by rain and tears and blood.

His memory of the attack is limited; a young man

hitting him with something large, a scuffle and then -
Where the hell is my phone?

His mind is becoming clear enough to panic. Bells. He can hear bells. Large and booming. Not a church. It's the clock in the market square, on the Council House.

He lies still. Listens and counts.

The melody plays out, one way, then in reverse, then back the other way.

11.45. Assuming he had only been unconscious a few minutes, instead of nearly an hour.

Oh God.

They'll be calling him. He said he'd give Michael until now, before he called them himself.

He tries to move. Can't. It hurts too much.

Maybe Michael did call them already. Perhaps that foolish narcissist actually did something the way he should, not the way he wanted too.

Ian lets himself believe this for a moment. It is a nice feeling.

Surely he did.

Surely.

Why wouldn't he? It's his money.

Relief.

A weight lifted. Like he himself is being raised up.

Pain courses through him, he cries out silently and his

head lolls, made dizzy again by the agony.

There are hands on him, pulling him, dragging him across the ground, away from this car. Voices, gruff and impatient, arguing with one another.

A car door opens and suddenly, with a final shove, accompanied by his own scream of torment, Ian is out of the rain and into the dry air of a car.

*

Camilla can see Travis's hand are shaking, either from the cold or from what he is seeing before him. She keeps her hands on him, though even to her, it is unclear whether it is to console him, or prevent him from leaving.

Travis's eyes travel across the bent form of the man, its head tilted away, that grotesque eye, popping out and staring back at them both.

'Travis - ,' she starts.

'Who is it?'

These are his first words for nearly a minute, and she chooses her own carefully, 'I thought he was a friend, but he tried to hurt me. I tried to get away, but he fell.'

Travis looks at her, worry in his eyes, 'He tried to hurt you?'

Camilla nods, unarmed by the genuine concern, 'He tried to rape me.'

Travis lets out a noise form his throat, like he has just been punched in the stomach. He grabs her arm, puts his hand on her cheek and searches her eyes, 'Did he..?'

'No,' Camilla shakes her head, 'No, it didn't get that far. But *this* happened and now I need your help. I need you to help me.'

Travis gulps deeply, and looks back at the body, but Camilla pulls his chin back to her, 'I need you to help *us*. Me. And your son.'

*

His heart thundering in his chest, Travis lets Camilla lead him back along the little corridor to the closed bedroom door. He stops by it, staring at it, suddenly terrified by the realisation that he has, for the first time in his life it feels, reached a goal.

'Go in,' Camilla says, soothingly, smiling. She leans across him, pushes the handle, and lets the door swing open.

The room smells of baby powder and the newly cut wood of flat-packed furniture. There is little in there; a small book case, a smattering of books on it, a chest of drawers with a pile of unopened baby-grows, a blue lamp on top casting a soft glow across the crib.

Travis can barely bring himself to step into the room, to cross it and peer into the cot. It takes all the courage he has left to do it, taking those strides, and placing his hand on the crib's edge.

His son stares back at him. Eyes wide and welcoming, his little mouth opening and closing, and tiny fingers that flex and curl and wave at him.

Travis's throat closes up and his eyes prickle. He reaches down with his finger and the baby grabs at it, pulling just for a moment. That instant is a spark that burns away all of Travis's selfish fear and cowardice and endless striving for that elusive easy way to get through life.

It is this little life that suddenly gives meaning to his own; his accidental, failed suicide attempt became contemptible. There is a new choice in his mind, one that has not been there before.

To give up his life to his own fear, or to give up his life for his child.

'Would you like to pick him up?' Camilla asks and Travis nods through his tears.

Camilla leans past him and picks the baby up, guiding Travis's arms and placing his son in them.

Travis stares down, as wide-eyed as the person staring

back at him.

'What's his name?' he asks.

Camilla shakes her head, 'He doesn't have one.'

'How can he not have a name?' Travis replies incredulously.

'Well, it doesn't make him any less of a person if he doesn't have a name!' Her tone is suddenly sharp, but she continues in a gentler voice, 'He'll want feeding soon. Do you want to do it?'

Travis nods quickly, staring at his son again. Camilla puts her hand on his arm and says, 'But first, we need to deal with our problem in the kitchen.'

*

The logistics of moving an inert human form are not something that Camilla has ever thought about before. For what seems like ages, both she and Travis stand at the edge of the kitchenette, staring down at the body.

The bleeding from the head and the awful mess of the eye socket has stopped, the one good eye is closed tight, the mouth open.

It is Travis who speaks first, 'Cammy, I don't know how to do this.'

Camilla may look frozen, but her mind is racing. To her

the clock on the kitchen wall is booming, not ticking. Every jerk of the second hand means her plans were that little bit closer to falling apart.

She closes her eyes. All she needs is a bit of luck and calm confidence, and within a few hours, she will be on a plane whilst the emergency services sift through the ash, trying to work out what the hell had happened, and Travis -

Camilla looks at him. What will happen to him afterward? What *had* happened to him tonight? He looks awful. As much as she resented what he was in her life, there was a shadow of feelings lurking at the back of her heart.

'Why did you need money?' she asks.

Travis tears his eyes off the body to look at her. After a moment he replies, 'It doesn't matter now.'

'Travis, what happened to you? Tell me,' she persists, only to receive a smile and shake of his head.

'Babe, it really doesn't matter anymore,' he says, 'I want you and the baby to be safe. That's all I want... after that...'

He trails off, his eyes wandering, but he clearly shakes whatever it is he is thinking away and asks, 'How do you want to do this? Because, I have no clue - '

Camilla scolds herself, brings herself back into the

present. She was about to fall into old ways. Looking after him.

No. He is no longer her problem.

It's about now. About her life. About getting it back.

The clock reads 11.50. There is no time for messing around.

'Grab his feet, We'll lift him onto this sheet, then I need you to drag him to the back door and put him in the big bins at the bottom.'

Travis baulks, 'In the alley? At the bottom of the stairs?'

'Yes.'

'What will you be doing?'

Camilla gives him the old, 'Are you an idiot?' look that he knows so well, 'I'll be cleaning up in here!'

Her sharpness jerks him into action, and she jabs her finger at the body, 'Travis. We need to do this now.'

Immediately, she grabs the aforementioned sheet, 'Lift him.'

Travis does as commanded, and together they go through a sequence of lifting Michael, tucking the sheet under and lifting him again until he is cradled in a white sack.

Camilla then grabs the edge by Michael's feet and holds the other edge out to Travis, 'Here.'

Travis takes it and copies her as she twists it round to

make an adequate handle.

Camilla tenses her arms, 'And pull!'

Together they heave. The surprise and disappointment in Camilla as she realises just how heavy a fully grown adult male is, comes out as a shrill, yet guttural cry.

The body slides off the linoleum onto the carpet whereupon friction makes the task even more difficult.

His face red, Travis heaves, along with Camilla, dragging the dead weight across the living room area by the flat's front door, to the back corridor. The floor here is exposed wood, and although easier than the carpet, is still significantly difficult.

As they pass the baby's room, a sound appears; high in pitch, strangled, wobbly.

Travis's face turns suddenly white as he looks down at the bloody bundle in horror. Camilla frowns and shakes her head in exasperation, 'It's the baby. He's hungry, remember?'

'Oh, okay,' he nods, relieved, 'Can I still feed him?'

Camilla half smiles, stress starting to put a strain on her friendly facade, 'Of course, just get this - '

An affable *tap tap tap* on the flat door cuts her off and they both look it.

Camilla swallows, gives Travis her best, and she feels, final, smile, 'Don't worry. It'll only be Sam. I'll sort it.

You get this down the back stairs, but don't come back in until I come to get you, okay?'

Travis thinks, clearly working the instructions through his head.

Camilla levels her gaze at him, 'Alright?'

'Okay,' he agrees and she walks away from him, then realises he has not moved. She turns and flicks a wrist urgently, 'Go on!'

He does, dragging the lump to the corner of the corridor alone, and out of sight.

Camilla walks quickly back to the kitchen. The clock says 11.53.

Fuck. Fuck. Fuck.

She grabs an Ikea rug that she had previously sorted and tosses it over the pool of blood. A few towels are draped over the edge of the sink to hide the droplets present, looking as if they are simply drying.

Camilla stands for a second, looks around. Her chest heaves with the pounding going on within. The Christmas tree sits, staring back at her. Waiting for its moment.

She needs to be out of here when that goes up. It'll be so fast, so violent. Everybody in this flat needs to be out by then.

Taking a breath, she crosses to the door.

15

Panic creases Cassandra's face as Ian's phone goes to voicemail again. Standing at the top of the stairs, by the door to the flat, phone in her hand, she feels out of control.

Where is he?

The only man she truly trusts has let her down.

She cancels the call, tries again. A succession of rings and his voicemail message echoes in her ear.

Goddammit!

The ten grand in her pockets suddenly feels light. They agreed a hundred K; the girl is immature, but not stupid. There is every chance she will get cold feet and back out if Cassandra can't prove that she can pay the full amount.

As she hangs up again, she checks the clock. Five to twelve. The deal should have been done by now. The money should have been transferred. Ian should have called.

Michael. He'd fucked it up again. On purpose? Who knew these days?

Sighing, Cassandra looks down and steels herself.

She is not leaving this flat without her baby.

The knock she presents to the door is as cheerful as she can muster, though it seems an age before it is opened.

Camilla smiles back at her broadly, 'Hi, Cassandra! Please come in, we're ready for you.'

Cassandra beams back at her, 'Oh, I'm so pleased. I'm so excited, honestly!'

Cassandra steps past Camilla, moving into the tiny flat. There is a smell in the air, earthy, metallic perhaps. A dirty, cramped place such as this, it could be anything.

Camilla skirts around her as she walks, as if to block her vaguely kitchen-bound trajectory.

Weird girl.

Camilla says, 'I don't want to hurry you, but I've been dodging work all night. Sam is getting suspicious, so I could do with making an appearance before very long.'

A little shard of concern hits Cassandra, 'Suspicious? How are you going to explain your baby's sudden disappearance?'

Camilla moves her weight from foot to foot, clearly agitated, wanting to move things along, 'It's fine. I have an explanation.'

Moving suddenly, Camilla grabs a small Tesco carrier bag, 'Here are a few things for you for tonight; a couple of made up bottles, a few vests and sleep-suits, nappies, wipes, nappy bags, all that jazz. I'm sure you're prepared, but it's just to make things easier for you.'

Cassandra is aware of how quickly Camilla is rattling things off. Urgency is radiating from her.

'Okay, lovely,' Cassandra replies, 'I really appreciate that.' She takes the carrier bag from Camilla and says, 'Then I suppose we'd better talk money.'

The relief that washes across Camilla's face abates Cassandras fears; she is desperate for the cash.

Camilla nods, 'Hundred grand.'

'Correct,' Cassandra replies and bites her lip as she continues, 'However.'

Camilla's face drops. She frowns.

'However?'

'There has been a delay.' Cassandra proceeds carefully. 'I was hoping to put around half in your hand, in cash, and transfer the remaining balance to you. However, and I assume there is simply a problem with the banks, it has not yet appeared.'

The fear in Camilla's eyes is evident and she asks evenly, 'So what are you saying?'

'I'm saying, that I have - ,' Cassandra fishes the envelope out of her purse, and offers it, ' -that I have £10,000 cash on me. The remaining ninety will follow within hours.'

Camilla says nothing. Does not take the envelope.

Cassandra continues, 'Now, as disappointed as I would be not to walk out of here with my baby, right now. I'm happy to wait for the money to appear. To give us both peace of mind.'

Camilla asks, her voice quieter, 'How long are we talking?'

'A few hours, perhaps.'

For some reason, Camilla looks straight across at the Christmas tree sat behind the chair and says nothing.

A moment passes. Cassandra feels the envelope getting lighter again. It's not enough. Panic starts to grip her.

She knows what she has to do, though God knows she doesn't want too.

Brightly, she says suddenly, 'Camilla, do you know what? I'm going to call Michael, see what the hold-up is.'

*

A Kiss At Midnight

Travis is standing at the top of the metal stairs, at his feet a dead man wrapped in a white bed sheet from Primark, and in his ears, 'Eye of the Tiger' by Survivor.

At first, he naturally assumes it is in his mind, his subconscious fighting to motivate him amidst this unspeakable and unprecedented situation. Travis hums along to his inner radio, while rain clatters off his t-shirt and soaks into the sheet, making the lump even heavier.

It is only when the illustrious chorus ends and the verses take over that he remembers that he does not know that many words to this song.

He pauses and listens. It is not in his head. It is coming from the white lump; from the body of the unknown man inside.

Travis kneels beside it, but cannot bring himself to reach inside. Instead, he moves the fabric aside, trying to keep the monstrous face covered.

The sound is coming from the man's suit jacket. Travis looks around, back through the open door. This Sam Camilla mentioned, he must be inside now with her.

Can they hear this? Will it draw their attention?

He has to deal with it; Camilla is depending on him to. He needs to prove himself to her again.

If he is honest with himself, he spent years letting her down. Making promises, breaking them, even when he tried to keep them. He simply made bad decisions; the promises were broken *for* him. No longer.

He has no idea how to sort the Baxter situation, even if he can. But right now, in this moment, he will make Camilla notice that he is now taking things seriously; at worst, if Baxter does catch up and kill him, at least Camilla will know that he would have been a good father.

If that's all he can give her and his son, it will be enough.

Travis plunges his hand inside, slips his fingers into the jacket, between the material and the still warm skin of the body.

There it is. Vibrating.

Pulling the expensive smartphone out, he looks at the name on the screen. Cassandra, and a photo of a slim, attractive woman he has never met. He presses the red cancel button.

Immediately it stops, and he goes through the routine of switching it off.

He slips the phone back into the man's inside pocket, then looks at the steps again.

They are very steep and slick with rain. How is he going to do this? They will struggle, even with two of them doing it.

Do it for Camilla.
Prove yourself.

Travis swings his arms and twitches his fingers.

Just get on with it. Just start, deal with things as they occur. That how you've always done it.

Travis grabs a handful of the sheet, straddles the body and heaves, dragging it towards the edge of the first step.

After much effort, the start of the bundle hangs over. Travis repositions himself so that he is behind it, then braces his back against the rails. Gripping the sheet tightly, placing his foot, he pushes.

It moves, inch by inch, until more and more of it is hanging over. He can feels weight shifting, pulling away from him.

Finally, it drops a little, shifting onto the first step. His arms ache. He allows himself to be pulled away from the rails, letting the lump settle a bit more, but still leaning back, he uses his foot to push again.

The body slides forwards once more, but this time does not settle on the next step. It tips, and the back end, closest to Travis, starts to overtake the front.

What might be the man's head and shoulder inside the sheet cocoon are rising above the legs, like the crest of a wave. It is ripping the hand-hold out of Travis's fingers.

Travis kicks out, trying to get the bottom to move, to get it to slide, not topple.

Success. It slides a little, but out of his control. Still

gripping it, he is yanked forward.

Two steps.

Three.

Then the wave again. The greater weight of the torso is dragged by gravity over the legs.

The lump crashes into the wall, turns and starts to roll like a ball.

Travis follows it, refusing to let go, until it is ripped from his grasp and all he can do is watch it topple, the body spilling from its sheet to the bottom, and crashing into the bins at the bottom.

The sound of the impact echoes through the narrow alley, reverberating back at him.

Travis doesn't move, waiting for the sound of anyone brought by the commotion. There is only the sound of bassy music from the bars and the aggressively jovial shouting of revellers on the surrounding streets.

No one comes.

Travis races down the steps, nearly tripping at the bottom. He crouches by the body in the wet gloom. The man is lying against the bin's caster wheels, on his hip, feet still on the steps. His face is pressed against the dirty metal side of the bin, a deluge of water is spattering on his cheek, spilling from a broken gutter above somewhere.

Travis sits back, on the bottom step, looking at the man's still face.

Ignoring the bulging eyeball, he looks kind, somehow. He doesn't look like a rapist. He just looks like a guy. Obviously, he had some money, lived a fairly luxurious life, and now he was dead, about to be dumped in a Nottingham city centre bin.

Travis shakes his head at the absurdity of it, until a thought strikes him.

He does look quite well to do.

Hurriedly, Travis looks around, then goes back into the man's jacket pocket. His clothes are twisted tight by the fall, but he is able to have good root around in all his pockets.

Nothing.

Not so much as a coin.

Travis sighs. Typical. He can never catch a break.

Standing, he opens the large lid of the bin and peers inside. Several black bags, one of which has ground-up food oozing out of a split, sit together like a dark mattress.

If getting him *down* the stairs was hard, getting him *up* into this bin was going to be a nightmare.

Again, just do it.

Travis leans over and grabs the man by his lapels and

stops, his heart in his mouth.

The bad eye bursting from his shattered socket stares sightlessly, but the other eye is now open and staring back at him.

It blinks.

16

Michael's voice inside Cassandra's ear makes her teeth grind, but she maintains her smile as Camilla looks on.

'Hi, you've reached Michael Clavell Associates. I'm not available to take your call, but please leave your name and number, and a brief message, and I'll get back to you, just as soon as I am able.'

There is a chime and silence. Cassandra looks at Camilla; her face has changed. She is nervous and edgy, not annoyed or irritated. She looks like she wants to run, not fight.

Why the fuck is Michael not answering!?

Camilla looks like she might change her mind about the sale.

I am not leaving without my baby. I will do whatever it takes.

A female computer voice speaks in Cassandra ear.

'If you'd like to rerecord your message, press 1.'

Camilla frowns, waiting.

Lie. Lie to restore confidence. Make her think everything is fine.

Not moving the phone from her ear, Cassandra suddenly smiles and speaks into the silence at the other end.

'Oh, Michael, I was starting to worry,' she says, then nods at the one way conversation, 'Yes, I'm here with her now. Uh-huh. Of course, I was just checking that everything is okay with the money? Oh, fantastic, I see. Okay then. Alright, I'll see you soon. Love you too.'

Cassandra presses the button to cancel the call that had already ended and gives Camilla her very best 'trust me' smile.

'Michael says everything is okay.'

*

Camilla hears the words, but it's like her world is suddenly filled with static. White-noise, obnoxiously loud, worse than the bass from the bar below, filling her ears, her mind, her whole existence.

Everything is okay.

Michael says everything is okay.

What the fuck is going on?

Camilla's legs suddenly feel weak. She stretches her hands out, gripping the side of the counter.

No, not that way.

Pushing herself away, she almost topples onto the arm of the white leather sofa.

Her vision fills with grey dots and she takes a deep breath, dragging air into her lungs.

'Are you okay?' A gentle voice, a slender hand on her shoulder.

Camilla looks up at the older woman. Her elegance, her sophistication, her grace, all seem so superficial after the lie. She looks deeper into the eyes that look down at her; yes, there. There is fear there, a fleck of it, hidden between the blues and greys of her iris.

Something is very wrong.

For whatever reason, there is no more money.

Camilla looks at Cassandra's hand, the envelope there, stuffed with the £10,000.

That's all there is. A fraction of what was agreed.

Not enough.

Camilla turns away. What is she supposed to do now?

The man she killed is behind her home, being hidden away by the father of her baby, who doesn't know that she is selling it.

He'll be back any minute. Travis will see the transaction, and he'll stop it.

£10,000.

It'll have to be enough. She needs to go now.

'Camilla?' Cassandra's voice is nervous. She cannot hide it. What if she backed out now?

Taking a breath, Camilla stands and states as confidently as she can, 'Ten grand now? The rest later... when it *arrives*?'

Cassandra nods slowly, 'Sure. Of course.'

'Then I'll go get your baby.'

*

Travis shifts to his right slowly, keeping his gaze on that second eye, then back to his left.

It's definitely following him.

He does a little left-right switch, jerky, unpredictable, and still Michael's one good eye follows him.

Shit. What does he do now? How can he be alive? That injury to his face, that fall down the steps...

'I'm in a lot of pain.'

The voice comes from nowhere. Michael's lips do not seem to have even moved.

Travis gulps, looks around.

'Please,' the voice comes again, 'please, help me.'

Looking down at the blood-streaked face, Travis can indeed see the faintest quivering of Michael's lips, his Adam's apple undulating slightly as he speaks.

'Please...'

'I don't know how...' Travis replies quickly.

Michael inhales loudly, rasping. How could they not have seen he was alive? Did Camilla not check? He certainly didn't.

Travis shakes his head, 'We thought you were dead.'

A faint smile crosses Michael's cracked lips, 'I know. I could hear, Travis. I could hear everything... I couldn't move...'

He trails off, winces, cries out silently, then continues, 'I was crying out, but you couldn't hear me. I think the fall woke me.'

'I'm sorry,' Travis utters, before realising who he has just apologised to. 'No. I'm not sorry. You deserve to be hurt after what you did.'

Michael, his eye closing sleepily, then opening again, says, 'I did nothing, Travis. You don't understand...'

His eye closes again, remains shut. Travis waits, but it

does not open. He crouches down quickly, shakes his shoulder.

'Ay. Ay, wake up. Understand what?' he asks when another question hits him. 'How do you know my name.'

Michael smiles, eye still closed, 'I know who you are, Travis. I've always known. You're the father.'

'What? How can you know that? I - '

'You don't understand,' Michael whispers, 'you don't understand... understand...'

Travis shakes him again, harder this time. Michael's eye snaps open, is confused, then seems to remember their conversation and where they left off, 'What time is?'

'Huh?'

'The time. What time is it?'

'I don't know; about ten to twelve, I think.'

Michael nods, 'There is still time.' He thinks, takes a few breaths, tries to move, but fails. After a moment, he speaks again, 'Camilla is trying to sell your son to my wife.'

Travis cannot understand; in this Michael is right. Sell his son? That doesn't make sense.

'What are you talking about?' Travis demands, 'She doesn't want to sell my son! She just let me see him. I'm going to go and feed him in a minute...'

He trails off at Michael's shaking head, 'I suspect that by the time you get back upstairs, my wife may already be there.'

Travis shakes his head, 'No. You're lying. I'm going to get Camilla - '

'Stop,' a bent hand suddenly shoots out from the side, grabbing at Travis, who is backing away, 'Listen to me! Listen!'

'Get off me!' Travis cries out, pulling away, but Michael keeps reaching.

'Travis, listen to me or we will both lose everything!' Michael hisses, his words slurred, his good eye rolling, trying to focus, 'I arranged the purchase, for my wife to buy your son... but I do not want it. Do you hear me? I was never going to go through with the sale.'

Travis stops, still sat on the steps, leaning away, listening.

'You can't buy a baby, Travis. There's too much of a paper-trail, too many records, between hospitals and registries,' Michael explains, 'I just needed them both to think it, but I wouldn't do that to someone like you. To a father.'

Travis takes in his words, head spinning, 'She was selling him?'

'Yes, with my money.'

Looking away, Travis tries to make sense of this new

development. Michael, getting seemingly stronger, reaches out and grabs Travis's hand, 'You need, money, Travis?'

Travis looks at him.

Michael grins, 'I know you do. I know you have trouble. I heard you. How much do you need?'

Travis whispers, 'Ten thousand.'

'I have a deal going through that is worth nearly half a million, Travis,' Michael says, his hand pawing at Travis, 'I can give you ten, maybe more. You can sort out your problem. You can start again, with your son. Help me.'

Travis thinks, then suddenly realises something, 'I have to stop them.'

He springs to his feet, stopping back up the steps. Michael calls after him, 'No! Wait!'

'I have to stop... the sale!'

'Travis, she has no money!'

Travis stops, looks back down at the crumpled form, 'You said you had half a million...'

'Not yet. Not yet. Cassandra has no money until I make the call.'

Travis looks around. He cannot get his head around all that is happening suddenly. Michael's voice, though raspy and pained, is slow and clear, 'I need to make a call, Travis. To arrange the deal, to get the money, but I will not give it to Cassandra. I will not buy your baby. I will give you your ten... but you need to help me. I'm running out time.'

Travis does not move.

'Help me.'

Sighing, Travis crawls back down the metal steps to Michael and kneels by him. Grinning, Michael speaks, 'Where is my phone?'

Travis thinks, then remembers, 'In your pocket!' He then starts fishing around, yanking the phone out, nearly dropping it.

'Go into the recent calls,' Michael instructs, 'Then show me the numbers. I'll tell you which one...'

Travis's face darkens.

Michael asks, 'What? What is it?'

Turning the phone to Michael, Travis reveals the smartphone's screen, shattered and warped with a rainbow stain spreading across the front.

'From the fall...' Travis mutters.

17

On the way to get the baby, Camilla looks around the corner of the rear corridor. The door is half open, rain still pouring down beyond the aperture.

She listens for movement, the sound of footsteps on the stairs or the banging of the bin's large lid.

Nothing.

Swallowing the fear that is creeping up her throat from her stomach, she slips into the baby's room.

He is awake, not crying, but make whimpering noises that Camilla has come to learn are a precursor to a full-on hunger tantrum.

Before she tends him, she goes to a shoulder bag sat on the nursing chair in the corner. It is her Go Bag, packed with all her very basics, all bought fresh, not from her drawers; underwear, a single change of clothes, toiletries. It waits patiently, ready to be taken as soon as her flat is empty of *all* unwanted guests.

Camilla takes the envelope that Cassandra has just given her, thick with twenty and fifty pound notes totalling ten thousand, and shoves it in the inner side pocket. She shoves deep down, but before removing her hand, gives it a final squeeze. Its thickness give her hope. It might not be much, but it's her new start.

Camilla leaves it and crosses to the cot. As she bends down over him, he looks up at her and lets out a mewing noise, little hands shaking, almost angrily. That's when the smell hits her.

Camilla sniffs, frowns and lifts his legs. A waft of putrid air hits her.

'For fuck sake,' she curses under her breath. This is the last thing she has time for.

Muttering, she grabs a nappy, a pack of wipes, and a nappy bag from the shelf above the cot, and begins frantically unbuttoning the bottom of the sleep suit.

With hands so deft and practised it continues to shock her, she hoists the sleep-suit over his waist and rips the self-adhesive tabs off the existing nappy.

Trying not to look at the deep brown smudge on the

inside, she wipes swiftly, until clear and drops them into the nappy before rolling it up.

It goes into the nappy bag and is sealed.

She pauses, listening for Travis returning, and hears nothing. As quickly as she can, she attaches a new nappy and re-buttons the sleep-suit.

Camilla picks the baby up, and is struck by a thought; that is the last time she will have to do that. No more cleaning up shit for her!

Relief washes over her, but as she turns, another smell wafts across her nostrils and she stops suddenly.

A sickly sweet smell, a blend of bottle formula and no more tears shampoo.

Camilla pauses, her baby in her arms. She can feel its breathing, a steady rhythm of contentment, arms curled up, head pressed against her chest.

The last of this too.

The last of any of it. She has resented the last several weeks; the night feeds, the constant interruption, the revolving of her life around it. Unable to live, only to serve this tiny tyrannical master.

And yet...

A bang on the flat door knocks her out of her unanticipated reverie, followed by the squeak and hiss of it being opened. Camilla feels her heart leap and she crosses to the door, looking out.

Cassandra is stood, facing the door, wide-eyed. It is Sam who stands leaning against it, his face ruddy, his brow furrowed. He stares at Cassandra and barks, 'I thought you'd left.'

Cassandra, reasserting herself, shakes her head and retorts coldly, 'No. I'm obviously still here.' She then glances over at Camilla, Sam's gaze following.

Camilla asks as casually as she can, 'What's wrong?'

'What's wrong?' Sam bellows and steps fully into the room, his large frame suddenly seeming to fill the flat, 'What's wrong is I have a bar full of customers and no one to fucking serve them, Camilla. What's wrong is that you've been up and down these fucking stairs all night playing with your new friends. What's wrong is that I need you downstairs, but beyond that, I've got four clowns in the bar asking to talk to you.'

Camilla doesn't understand what he is saying, 'Who's downstairs?'

Sam sighs heavily, 'Four blokes who say they want to talk to you about Travis. Something I need to do know?'

Camilla's mind goes into hyper-mode. The Christmas tree in the corner is ready to go off; the clock on the wall reads 11.52. Travis is out back somewhere. Cassandra is waiting on her baby. If Sam realises any of what is happening, he'll put a stop to everything.

Bastard. Every time Camilla thinks she has a handle on things, Sam appears and fucks them up again.

Think.

Get rid of these 'clowns', tell them you haven't seen Travis.

Next give Cassandra the baby, and get her out of the front door.

Shove Travis out of the back door again.

Get out and get to the airport with Cassandra's ten grand.

All in eight minutes.

'Okay, I'm coming,' Camilla shouts back, trying to sound angry to hide her fear. She crosses to Cassandra, passes the baby over to her, leaning in as she does and whispers, 'I will be back in *one* minute.'

Cassandra, barely taking her eyes off her baby, nods. Camilla sighs heavily and motions grumpily at the door for Sam, 'Come on then!'

*

The flat door whooshes shut and the flat is suddenly quieter, save for the thudding of the music below.

Cassandra stands, a feeling of victory passing through

her; her prize sits lightly in her arms, staring up at her.

She looks back, her heart so full she feels it might explode; he is hers, finally and irreversibly hers.

Cassandra can restrain herself no longer and leans down to plant a tender kiss on his forehead.

Immediately, he starts to cry. A shrill warble that cuts through the relative silence of the space.

Cassandra's throat closes up. She feels as if her heart genuinely and physically breaks a little.

He hates me.

He knows I am not his true mother.

She stares at his face, warped with bantam fury, belting out his song of anguish.

Cassandra starts to coo and soothe, bouncing him up and down a little, rocking back and forth. It does nothing, expect make him worse.

She looks around, searching for an idea of what might be wrong with him. Craning her neck painfully, she sniffs his backside, but detects nothing.

Hungry?

Cassandra's eyes fly around the room before spotting the Tesco carrier bag on the floor by the kitchen. She reaches inside and finds a baby's bottle, still slightly warm from when it was made.

Shushing as gently as she can, Cassandra struggles to

use a manicured nail to pop the lid off. Her nail cracks before the lid gives and she swears, shaking the lid away.

Frantically, she plunges the bottle's teat into the gaping hole. Straight away, lips closes around it and the screaming is replaced by frenzied sucking and guzzling noises.

Cassandra is overwhelmed by a feeling of self-satisfaction and peace; it is intoxicating. She moves to sit down on the sofa, but they look too soft; she wants support, not used to holding a baby for any period of time.

The chair by the small window is a better option.

Cassandra sits down and settles in, staring happily down at the baby draining its bottle, ounce by ounce.

The fir branches of the old, dried Christmas tree behind her tickle her neck, but she ignores both it and the low ticking sound coming from behind her, as she gazes into the sweet eyes of her future.

18

If getting a dead body down a set of stairs is difficult, getting a wounded, live one, who complained and fidgeted, back up them seems impossible.

Travis's arms, hooked under Michael's armpits, burn as he heaves the nearly inert lump skyward. A single man, fighting an entire planet's gravity, but foot by foot, inch by inch, he is gradually winning.

Michael is muttering continuously, most of it barely comprehensible. Travis can make out the odd name he knows; Camilla, Cassandra, and another name, Ian. He speaks a lot about Ian; 'Ian will sort it, he's a good man, a good friend, he'll fix it, he always does.'

Soaked and exhausted, Travis uses the last of his

strength to drag Michael across the top step, and with a clang, dumps him. Travis falls down beside him, breathing hard, the muscles in his arms and legs throbbing.

He lifts his head to look at Michael. The man's bulging eyeball looks even more grotesque than it did before; it might even have slid further from the socket. It seems to rock a little as Michael shakes from the cold and shock.

Swallowing sudden nausea, Travis looks away and steals himself. The hard bit is over. They just need to get down the hallway, into the flat itself, and find Michael a phone.

One call, and Travis can pay Baxter, stop the sale, and build a life with his son.

The prospect is blindingly glorious and his chest swells with hope for it.

'Come on,' he breathes, pushing himself up painfully.

Michael doesn't answer, both eyes locked and frozen, so Travis grabs his shoulder. Instantly, Michael's good eye swivels to him.

Travis says, 'We have to go, okay? Can you move yet?'

Michael looks down his body, trying to will something to move; his left arm jerks, left leg twitches, but the exertion showing on Michael's face says that will be all.

Travis is no doctor, but even he can tell that something is really very wrong inside the injured man.

Grabbing Michael's good arm, hooking it over his shoulder, he stands. Feeble-framed, it takes Travis more than he has to find a stance with which to drag Michael back through the heavy back door.

'Good man... you're a good man... Travis,' Michael mutters as they move slowly, 'I will sort you out, I will. We'll end this together. What work do you do?'

Grunting, Travis answers, 'I play guitar.'

Michael spits, 'No money in that. Not in the long... long term... what work do you do?'

'Nothing,' Travis replies, finally finding his way out of the rain again, 'I tried to buy a burger van with my mate.... but that went... wrong.'

Michael makes professional affirmation noises, punctuated with a decrepit gasping rattle, 'I see, that's why you owe the money.'

Travis heaves Michael's dragging feet around the door frame, using the plastered walls for support, 'Yeah, that's right.'

'I will... I will sort you out, Travis. For this, for doing this... this... I will sort you out a job. You'll work for me... I see you right, you and your boy... I was a killer businessman, Trav... Travis... I will be again... we'll get you set up and see...'

In that moment, Michael suddenly gets heavier, and

Travis strains all the more. He takes another step, but the weight is now too much for him.

He sinks to the floor, grimacing.

Damnit, he's passed out. How's he supposed to call to confirm this deal now?

Travis, half pinned beneath Michael, mumbles expletives under his breath. *Again! A promise of something, snatched away again.*

Furious at the fates, Travis shakes himself free of the arm and turns to face Michael.

Michael's bulging eyeball stares away from him, the other eye gazes back at him, wide, sightless.

Travis shakes him again, and the jaw drops open, the head lolling back awkwardly.

There is no one in there.

The thought hits Travis hard and he lets go instinctively. Michael flops backwards, his head hitting the wall, forcing his chin into his chest at an unnatural angle.

Travis, mouth open, backs away.

Christ, he was talking... he was there and then... he wasn't. He was just...

Gone...

The corridor is silent but for the drumming of the rain on the metal steps, two men lying in the dark hallway. One dead, one alive, and knowing he will soon join the other in slumber.

Travis presses his face into his hands. This is his life, hope followed by disappointment, an eternal rollercoaster that, with each successive dip, falls lower and lower.

There is only so deep it can go until it must end.

That end must be close.

Heavy darkness closes around him.

Pitch black.

Endless, complete and silent.

No, not silent.

There is a sound. A shrill wailing. It warbles and coos, a hard cry coming from beyond the darkness.

Beyond the corridor.

From the flat.

Suddenly, Travis is on his feet, stumbling over the dead body and hurrying along the dimly lit hallway.

Light before him, a room on his left. The smell of talcum powder and perfumed faeces waft out at him; the cot is empty.

Travis rushes past it, bursting into the flat's main room, and looks around frantically.

There he is, cradled in arms, a fresh bottle between his lips, cooing softly.

Travis's gaze drifts up, locking eyes with the woman

holding his son. The woman who is not his son's mother. Her own eyes widen with a mix of surprise, fear and anger.

He knows who she is.

And she knows who he is.

*

The bar is as busy as when Camilla left it, if not even busier. Usually the rain keeps people indoors, but tonight the heavens had not opened until well past 8pm. Most people will have already been out by then, mentally and physically committed to their drinking plans. They will blame the rain for keeping them inside the pubs, drinking on and on until the rain eases, if it ever will. In reality, the decision is their own, but they will never accept responsibility for it. Why should they?

Sam barges the bottom door open, a surge of noise sweeping over Camilla. He is furious with her. She can tell, as it is such a contrast from how he usually is with her. Generally, she gets away with murder, and that makes her unpopular with her co-workers.

Tonight, however, something is bothering him. Something more than Camilla's lackadaisical attitude to work.

Still, she won't be seen to be repentant. Not tonight of all nights. What Sam had coming was of his own making. With the most tired and indignant tone she can muster, she demands, 'Where are they, then?'

Sam stops, stares at her for a moment. His gaze projects a blend of anger and genuine disappointment; they say, 'I don't know who you are any more.'

For a heartbeat, Camilla's resolve falters, but she catches herself.

There is ten grand cash upstairs for her. And no baby tying her down.

She gives Sam an arrogant shrug. *Go on then!*

Sam grunts, 'Those lot over in the booth. Get rid of them, get rid of your mate upstairs and get the fuck back down here and serve!'

Without another word, Sam turns and marches back to the bar to start work on the crowd pressing up against it.

Camilla, irritated by his tone watches him go. *Arrogant twat, he has no idea what's coming.*

She glances at the big neon clock on the wall: 11.56.

Shit. She'd better make this bloody quick.

Camilla turns and pushes her way through the heaving crowds, nudging past groups laughing and cheering, isolated introverts sipping through straws, pairs of predatory extroverts stalking salaciously.

Of the three booths the bar has, the first has only a couple in there; the gangly, spiky haired male nibbling on his girlfriend's ear across the table; the second has three people, all males.

Camilla stops, looking expectantly at them, 'What do you want?'

All three pairs of eyes go to her, surprised and unsure; long, stringy beards and Steel Panther t-shirts, obscure craft ales sold in 2/3rd pints the subject of their conversation.

None of them reply.

'Over here, bro.'

The voice is rough, and comes from her right, the next booth over.

Camilla turns and sees a man, waving enthusiastically at her. He is broad-shouldered, bearded, with some form of abnormality on his upper lip. He keeps smiling, and she frowns, stepping over.

Cut Lip grins up at her, 'Alright, bro? You Camilla?'

Camilla looks across the table. There are three other men, two looking similar to Cut Lip, but one clearly having at least partly south-east Asian origins. Both of them look at her.

The third man has very dark skin, and is slim but clearly muscular. His eyes are dark and intense under his

hooded top, even as he stares down at his vodka coke.
For some reason, she hopes he won't look at her.
Replying to Cut Lip, she says sharply, in her best barmaid tone, 'I am, but don't call me *bro*, sunshine.'
Cut Lip laughs suddenly, loudly, but genuinely. He looks around at his cohorts, who join in. The fourth man does not.
'Love it,' Cut Lip says through his laughter, 'I knew you'd be a right pistol. I could tell, right off the bat.'
Camilla nods, smiling, but she ensures that it comes across as insincere, 'So, what do you want?'
Cut Lip's smile fades, 'Alright, listen... darling. I want to talk our mate.'
'What mate?' Camilla replies curtly.
Cut Lip rolls his eyes, looking at his well-trained posse, who echo the mannerism, 'Our mate Travis.'
Camilla mind goes to Travis, right now dumping Michael's body in the big bin behind the bar.
Time. Minutes left. Get rid of these wannabe gangsters.
'Haven't seen him,' she states, 'I don't know what he's been telling you, but I haven't seen him in over a year.'
Cut Lip bursts into aggressive laughter, waving his hand for mercy like he's watching Live at the Apollo, 'No, no. Don't start that. I've been watching him fucking about, in and out of here, all fucking evening. Don't spin me

that shit, bro. Sorry, *sweetheart.*'

Camilla, her heart suddenly starting to thud, says, 'Look, he might have been here, but he ain't spoken to me. I haven't seen him.'

At the end of the table, the black man shifts in his seat, and exhales. His fingernails tap his glass.

Cut Lip glances over at him, and suddenly his cheerful demeanour alters. He levels a very serious gaze at Camilla, 'Okay, I'm going to be straight with you. I'm in trouble with the boss-man here. I was supposed to keep an eye on Trav; make sure he paid his debt, right?'

Camilla keeps her expression neutral. Debt. These are the people he owes money to. She should have guessed earlier, but her mind was a little distracted with other, more pressing issues.

Damnit, she needs to get away from this conversation. Has to have been nearly two minutes now.

Fuck!

It isn't going to happen. She needs to get back upstairs and cancel the timer. Reset it. Just half an hour will do. Slam the back door on Travis, take the money, and sneak Cassandra and the baby out the front.

But she needs to get rid of this lot first. What will they do to Travis? They just want their money, they won't hurt him, at least not too badly. Not until they get their money.

Okay, tell them. Tell them he's out back. That'll free you up to sort the timer and Cassandra out. Take the 10k, get out, and when Cassandra pays the remaining ninety grand, give Travis whatever he needs to get him out of this mess. Fuck it, she can afford it. Save him, one last time, then be done with him once and for all.

Camilla sighs heavily, disingenuously, 'Yeah, okay. He's here.'

The black man suddenly turns and looks at her, right through her. A chill courses through her.

'Great,' Cut Lip says, 'Glad to see we're getting somewhere. Sit down.'

Camilla frowns, 'I just told you. He's here. He's round the back, in the alley.'

'Good stuff, thanks,' he nods at the other two men. They stand immediately and head for the door. Cut Lip smiles again, nodding at the empty seats, 'NO, I said sit.'

'Please,' Camilla says, 'I really need to get back upstairs. Straight away.'

Cut Lip holds up his hand, 'Just, hang on. You will. There's no rush.'

'Please..!'

Sighing, Cut Lip pulls his jacket open a little so that she can see the handle of a handgun, tucked in just out of sight.

Camilla's heart climbs into her throat, and chokes her there as Cut Lip smiles once more.

'Now, I said sit... and relax.'

19

Cassandra's moment of peace and contentment is shattered by the sight of the scruffy young man with a shock of soaking, ginger hair. Water runs off his coat in rivulets, from his shoes, and dribbles down his wobbling chin, creating a wet patch around him on the wooden floor.

His hazel eyes are burning pits of fury, steady and unblinking. Fists, clenched at his sides. Breathing, hard, but even.

Cassandra is unafraid. Not because she is brave, but because she has come too far to get here. Done and given up too much, not just tonight, but throughout her life. She pulls the baby closer to her. The movement, territorial in its intent, incites a physical response in Travis. He jerks forward a fraction.

Cassandra returns his gaze with her own, equally firm and unrelenting. She will not give up the baby. It is her reward, long awaited and hard won.

For years, she searched for her way forward, upward. From her working-class roots, dragged up by her loveless mother in a rotting southern council estate. From her mid-teens, she discovered that she was desirable; tall and slim, she naturally had the body and looks that her female friends coveted, and her male friends craved. The former eventually resented her, actively shunning her, especially when she began to encourage the interest of the latter. She was popular, but even at that young age, she knew they were not what she wanted. Not what she needed to escape the filth-ridden alleys and shopping centres of her childhood.

Two decades of pursuing men of power, and more importantly, wealth, saw her body ravaged outwardly by alcohol and drugs. Inwardly, she grew hard, knowing she was being used, but accepted it as part of the greater journey. Her path, with each sexual encounter, each progressive pickup and rejection, was pushing her further along. There were disappointments, men who wanted her deeply, but had very little, and those who had it all, but wanted her for nothing more than a single night. Eventually, she had found Michael; attractive, confident and with a wealth that seemed ever-increasing.

For several years, she finally had everything she wanted. A stunning house in an enviable area, an expensive car, clothes, jewellery. Where her childhood compatriots were still struggling to top up the electricity meter and fill their fridges with anything beyond takeaway leftovers, she found herself barely using her double-door fridge, opting to eat out more often than not.

It was when Michael suddenly seemed to lose his Midas touch, when the shadowy threat of losing everything loomed over her, that her desires changed.

She has never loved Michael. She had had too many men treat her badly, and treated them equally as awfully, to ever be capable of loving one.

But she wants to love. To give it utterly and unconditionally, and far more importantly... to have it returned.

Genuine love. Unquestionable affection. Eternally.

This can only come from a child.

Decades of physical abuse ruined her body, not just at the hands of barmen, dealers and fellow junkies, but by the surgeons who had performed the five abortions that had eventually annihilated her uterus.

A Kiss At Midnight

Cassandra can attest that there is no state of hell worse than to be a mother without a child. She is already *mum*, but has no one to call her that.

She refuses to adopt. That will incite questions about her dark history from her current crop of well-to-do coffee shop 'friends'.

Cassandra needs to have her own, somehow.

And Michael, though on the verge of becoming useless to her, could well perform one final task for her. He will be easily motivated, and she knows exactly how. To the amateur armchair psychologist, Michael is an archetypal sex-fiend, but it is *not* about that at all. Sure, he wants and enjoys physical pleasure, but that was not what turns him on. For him, she had long worked out, his passion for sex is the same as what drives his entrepreneurial work; domination and supremacy.

To deny him sex, is not about sex. It is about removing the power from him, and making him earn it back.

Once tonight is over, and she puts her baby to bed in her lavish home, she will reward him with her body. Within days however, she will be piling his bags up on the front lawn, so to speak.

First however, she has to deal with this little ginger turd. He is in her way, and no man stays in her way for long.

Travis speaks first, with a predictable opener, his voice

shaky with anger, 'Give me my son.'

Cassandra, keeping the bottle steady in the baby's mouth, answers slowly, evenly, 'I challenge you to provide any documentation that proves that, Travis.'

The young man gulps, blinking, thinking, 'I'm on the birth certificate - '

Cassandra smirks, leaning forward, 'Are you?'

Travis frowns, troubled.

In the kitchen, the clock on the wall lets out a little noise, a faint *ting-ting*.

Outside the window, the giant clock on the council house dome, seemingly inspired by its far smaller cousin, begins to boom out its message.

Midnight.

*

There is the faintest click from behind the chair on which Cassandra and the baby sit.

It either goes unheard, or ignored by them both.

Travis, his mind whirling, trying to order his thoughts, thinks clearly, and suddenly says, 'I will fight you.'

Cassandra scoffs at him, making his blood boil, 'Do you mean now? With your fists? Attack a mother and her baby? Or in the courts? That costs money, Travis; do you have much in the way of that? Because I do.'

Her smile is beautiful and severe, filled with confidence and dominance; it crackles and hisses as it sucks air in to power it. And she is suddenly framed with light and heat. She opens her mouth to speak again, to ridicule him further, to crush him, diminish him, but seems to feel the heat on the back of her head.

As she turns, a column a fire rises up, swallowing the old dried Christmas tree, turning it to ash almost instantly. It does not resist, seems to relish its swift demise. Months of standing behind that chair, drying up, gradually decaying but death never fully coming.

There is a terrific roar, staccato at first, then a symphony of branches igniting, pockets of air and sap exploding.

Travis takes an instinctive step backwards, eyes wide in terror, as flames break across the ceiling like ocean waves on a cliff face. They spread out, gushing along the thin wood and plaster, a fiery, inverted tidal wave over his head.

Travis falls to the floor, ducking away from the flames licking the top of his hair.

Mere seconds have passed, but already the tree is gone, replaced by a wall of fire, spreading up and outwards. The curtains are burning shreds, the walls are cracked with veins of heat, curling flames working their way swiftly around the room.

Travis has never felt such primal dread, not even when faced with the drill in Baxter's hand. At least that was guided by a human mind, malicious though it was. This demonic fire is unknowable and irrational; it cannot be reasoned with. It will consume without mercy.

Destroy.

Kill.

His son.

The thought hits him with less than ten seconds having gone by, but it seems like hours. Guilt hits him. How can he have forgotten?

Tremendous heat washes across him, and he holds his hand up over his face. There they are. Cassandra, clutching the baby to her chest, has fallen away from the chair. The chair itself is now engulfed in curling flames that seem to reach out for her.

She is on her side on the floor, baby held tight. The hair at the back her head is alight, tiny flames climbing up towards her scalp.

Cassandra wriggles, with her arms busy, she kicks out at the chair, trying to push herself away from it. Her foot hits the chair leg, twice, four times, each instance propelling her a few inches away from the inferno towering over her.

The fifth impact snaps the leg and the burning chair collapses onto her bare ankle.

Travis watches Cassandra cry out. She lets go of the baby with one arm, and uses her free one to push at the chair seat. It is too hot, and she lets go.

He has to help her, to help his son.

Keeping low, he moves towards her.

She sees him coming, shoots him a look, not of thanks, but of 'stay away'. Cassandra reaches over her head, grabs the edge of a counter's post and, with a cry, pulls herself up.

Her foot, already blistering, slides out from under the chair, and she drags herself into the kitchen area, out of sight.

Travis, relieved that they are out of immediate danger, changes his trajectory. He heaves himself up onto his haunches and scuttles along to the breakfast bar that separates the living area from the kitchen.

Once there, he grabs onto the counter's top edge and rises up. The heat bearing down on him from the sea of flames above is unbearable.

He looks around the living area. The entire far wall is awash with flames. The TV stand, the lamp, and the far end of the sofa is already burning. The rug is ablaze, the cheap fabric burning rapidly.

How can it be this bad already?
Turning his attention back to his son, Travis rises against the heat and peers over the top of the counter.

Cassandra is sat on the floor, propped up against the cupboard door. She is frantically patting the fire on the back of her head, extinguishing it with her bare hand. The baby, bottle now utterly lost, is screeching and wailing.

Travis thrusts his hand on the worktop at her, 'Come on! This way!'

Cassandra looks up at him with a coldness that might challenge the inferno around them and screams back at him, 'Fuck you!'

Travis feels the top of his head beginning to scorch, and the air around them is rapidly becoming hot. Behind him, the sofa is now entirely overcome with fire, blasting him with intense heat.

He leans over, pleading with her, 'Please! Just let me get my son out of here!'

Suddenly, the curtain rail falls and tips into the kitchen, spreading fire towards them. Cassandra screams, adding to the baby's increasing shrieks. She scampers away, then looks at Travis, and makes a decision.

She bundles up the baby, braces against the heat, and throws herself bodily across the counter, at Travis.

But not before, as Travis realises too late, she snatches a large blade from the spilled knife block.

20

The sound of the council house clock chiming is the sound Camilla always hoped to hear from the train station, just as she boarded. Or at the very least, from down the street, as she walked away, alone and several thousand pounds richer.

Instead, she is sat at a table with two dangerous men, one of whom is concealing a gun.

The gongs are audible as the bouncer opens the door; three almighty booms, lost as soon as the door is closed. But Camilla can still hear them in her head.

She can only imagine what is happening upstairs at this moment; Cassandra is up there, Travis is up there, and her baby is up there.

Camilla risks a look around, towards the door, then at the ceiling above her. She can see nothing, hear nothing, and smell nothing.

Maybe it didn't work. Perhaps it failed. She is no professional arsonist after all.

Cut Lip sneers, 'Looks like Travis's time is up.'

Camilla looks over at him, but she doesn't see him. Her mind is upstairs, trying to envision the events unfolding upstairs.

Seconds pass.

Still nothing. No smoke. No alarm.

It didn't work.

Relief.

Then it begins to rain indoors. A flash flood falling from the ceiling. Cut Lip's horrible grin vanishes as he is instantly soaked, and Baxter, stoic until now, jumps and looks around in surprise.

Then the alarm sounds, a shrill pulsing buzzer.

The room full of people, once segregated into organic groups and pairs, suddenly becomes a heaving amalgam of screaming and shoving.

The chaos that ensues sweeps across the bar quicker than the fire raging out of sight up stairs. It becomes a single, writhing organism, wet and wriggling, squirming towards the door. It spills across the table where Camilla sits with her captors. Someone is thrown against the surface, another loses their footing and is pulled under by sheer force of survival.

Camilla is frozen at first, watching the consequences of her actions, for the first time understanding the ramifications of her decision.

Her eyes drift down. A young woman with rainbow hair and a skinny frame is drowning beneath heavy feet; she cries out, terrified, pinned down. A stiletto heel, on the end of a stumbling, unsteady leg, crashes unknowingly into the girl's cheek.

Her scream is lost in the sound of trampling feet, the sight of her blocked by wet, twisting bodies.

Camilla can only stare as her frightened face disappears.
What have I done?
To these people?
To my baby?
A switch is flicked in Camilla's mind. Before she knows it, she is throwing herself into the sea of bodies.

Cut Lip sees her go, whips a hand over to grab her but misses.

Camilla, smaller than he, slips between the rushing people but the far larger man is trapped in the booth.

She struggles against the current, pushing and shoving, clawing her away to the back as everyone else struggles to the front. An elbow crashes into her cheekbone, a light flashes, someone scrapes her bare shoulder, and someone else winds her.

Then there is a voice, her name called out, 'Camilla! Camilla, where are you going?'

She looks over, and sees a head above the bodies, waving at her. It is Sam, worry scrawled across his face.

Camilla's throat closes, tight with regret, 'I'm sorry, Sam! I'm so sorry!'

Sam calls back, waving furiously, 'What? Camilla, come this way! The fire service is - '

She can hear no more. Camilla turns and pulls her way free of the crowd that is sprawling across the empty bar floor. The door is ahead of her, and she runs to it. Yanks it open.

The stairway is clear. No smoke or fire.

Camilla pounds up them as fast as she can, slipping from her wet shoes, smashing her knees on the steps. Reaching the top, she puts her hand on the door handle.

It is warm.

Panic rushes over her; violent, overwhelming panic, that makes her shake uncontrollably. Her vision swims, her head pounds.

She pushes the door open and hot air pushes back at her.

Camilla gasps, both from the sudden change in atmosphere and the sight.

She has walked directly into hell.

Flames climb the walls, a tide of fire flows across the ceiling; everything is flooded in a blinding, red-orange glow. The roar of the inferno is deafening and the stench of her life burning away to ash makes her choke.

She drops to her knees. A cloud of black smoke is forming at the top of the room, filling it, forcing it to sink towards her.

She looks around, squinting through the brightness and heat. What was once her living room is nothing but fire; nothing is recognisable and her kitchen is swiftly being swept away. There is no one here. No one alive anyway.

The cloud of smog drops and engulfs her. She takes a breath without meaning to and swallows a lungful of the thick smoke. She coughs explosively. Her chest burns agonisingly.

Camilla turns and crawls away, to the corridor, feeling her way along the wall until she reaches the baby's room. She looks inside and finds it empty.

The smoke follows her and although she tries to hold her breath, her crippling panic forces her to take a deep lungful of the noxious air.

She cries out in pain, clutching her chest, and drops to

her stomach, trying to stay under the black cloud, inches above her.

Camilla looks at the cot, pulls herself towards it, foot by foot, until she is alongside it. She grips the slender bars, heaves herself up to look inside.

There is a lump there and she cries out in terror. Reaching between the bars, she pulls at the blanket, revealing nothing. It was only the bedsheets bunched up. Where is he? Where is her baby?

She thinks of him. Alone. Crying and terrified. Slowly suffocating to death. Calling out for his mother who never told him that she loved him. Who never wanted him, who was giving him up for money, for a life that she had lost.

Tears pour from her eyes, bitter regret and self-hatred. She lets out a wail of despair.

There is a wail in reply. Shrill warbling, faint, but there.

Camilla's eyes, red and blurry with smoke, snap open and she listens, trying to not cough.

There again. A cry she would know anywhere. It's coming from outside the window, from the metal fire escape at the back. Another voice too, male, shouting.

Travis.

Camilla laughs, joy and relief filling her heart. Travis is with him. Travis has his son. They are alive together.

Camilla looks at the doorway beyond her feet. Through the smoke, she can see the fire creeping along the hallway, licking at the nursery's door frame.

She breathes in involuntarily, gets a lungful of putrid air, and chokes.

Grabbing the blanket from the cot, she presses it against her mouth and nose, and inhales. The sweet scent of baby powder and shampoo fills her head and she is suddenly no longer lying on the floor of a burning building.

Camilla sits in the chair, her son in her arms, gazing up at her with his soft, grey-green eyes. He sucks softly on the bottle, utterly content and wanting for nothing more. She feels his breathing, soft and steady, going on and on, and she holds him as tight as she dares, simply feeling his presence and loving him.

Her eyes close tight against the smoke. Camilla breathes through the baby blanket, and in her mind, repeats a name.

Her son's name.

She has never told it to anyone, never said it aloud, or even truly acknowledged it to herself lest she become attached.

But he has one.

He has always had a name.

And it is the last word her mind ever thinks.

*

Cassandra tumbles around the corridor's sharp corner, banging into the wall shoulder first. She tries to protect the baby from the impact, but feels it shudder through them both, causing the tiny being to cry even harder.

Thick black smoke pursues her, clinging to the ceiling, pushing ever further.

Looking back briefly, Cassandra peers into the dark fog, the crackling orange beyond it. She can see nothing, hear no one.

She pushes herself off the wall just as the smog envelops her, smothering her vision.

Stumbling on, using both hands to hold her prize, brushing the wall with her shoulder to guide her, she moves towards the end. A light there, sodium orange and the sound of heavy pellets of water hitting the metal.

Escape.

Freedom.

She goes down hard. So hard, she barely has time to react, to turn her body away so that she lands on her shoulder badly.

Crying out as pain shoots through her, she is suddenly

aware that the baby has stopped crying.

Oh dear God; I've crushed him...

Rocking onto to her back, she looks down at him. His eyes are screwed shut, but his mouth is moving. He coughs, choking on the smoke.

She has to get out or she will lose him.

Cassandra kicks out, pushing herself against the unseen hazard that had tripped her. The smoke clears just enough for her to see it.

An eye stares back at her. Not a normal eye, it is loose from its socket, bulging out, devoid of protective eyelids, wide and dead.

And it belongs to Michael.

She opens her mouth, to scream in surprise, but finds the sound does not appear. Although the sight of him shocks her, in this state, she is not saddened by it. In these few seconds, she feels only the briefest sliver of remorse; they had shared some good times together, she had in truth enjoyed his company and his companionship more than she had with any other man in her life, but he had become a burden.

She knows it is horrid, but this is the best possible outcome for her.

She looks away from his ghastly, disfigured face and starts to pick herself back up, to run for the pouring rain beyond the aperture.

She gets to her knees when she hears a voice bellowing out from behind her.

'Give me back my son!'

22

In reality, Travis and Camilla have missed each other by only three seconds. Clutching his bleeding hip, perforated by the knife Cassandra had thrust at him, Travis stumbles by the flat's entrance and moves into the corridor, under the cover of the smoke just as Camilla opens the door to hell.

Whilst her attention is taken by the sight of her life burning around her, Travis stumbles along the corridor to the L and catches sight of Cassandra lying on the floor beside her late husband. In her arms, his son, crying and coughing painfully.

Wrath flares up in him and he bellows across at her, 'Give me back my son!'

He sees her head snap towards him, surprise replaced quickly by her own, equal anger. Standing unsteadily, baby in her arms, she shouts back, 'He's not your son. In the eyes of the law, he never was.'

Travis, unafraid, fuelled by protective instinct, marches on her, fists clenched. He will take back his son. He will do anything to do it.

Clearly, this intention radiates from him, as Cassandra instantly turns and flees out of the open doorway.

Despite his side burning, feeling like it is ripping apart with every stride, Travis races after her and throws himself out into the rain.

Cassandra is gone.

His head jerks left and right, around, looking for her. She is not descending the stairs, and she certainly did not leap over the fifteen foot drop from the top, least of all with a baby in her arms.

A clatter behind him and he looks up into the rain, at the various levels of rooftop rising up behind the flat and the bar.

Her hair drenched, matted to her face, Cassandra peers back at him from above. She has somehow climbed the air conditioning unit and up onto the steep tiles of the flat's pitched roof.

What the hell? Why did she not just go down the stairs?

Travis looks down and sees people, a dozen or so, crowding along the generally empty alleyway. She doesn't want to be seen, to cause a fuss. If Travis starts shouting the odds about her stealing his son, it will turn heads, provoke questions.

He is about to start doing that very thing, when a face in the crowd suddenly looks directly at him. It is a face he recognises.

Bearded chin, with a cut on his upper lip. He smiles upon seeing Travis, and gives a cheerful wave.

Travis's heart drops to his stomach. There are three other men with him, and the fourth also looks up at him. Looks him directly in the eye.

Baxter.

The hammering of the rain suddenly becomes the scream of a drill, and Travis knows he has no choice.

*

After negotiating the steep, slippery, tiled roof, Cassandra heaves herself onto the flat surface of the next building. The rain seems harder up here, the drops heavier, the air far colder.

She pulls the baby closer, tries to tuck him under her long coat. Having been a mother for all of ten minutes, she can do without having to deal with an infant cold on her first night.

Cassandra walks quickly, hoping that if she can hop up onto the Marks and Spencer roof, she can find a fire escape on the far side somewhere. That should allow her to drop back down onto Pepper Street. From there she can work her way back around to her car. If things go her way, she can be home by 1am. She can get dry, pour a glass of wine and put her baby to sleep.

She envisions the morning. Waking peacefully, hearing the gentle breathing of her child, she'll make coffee and feed him his bottle on the covered decking. Later, she'll put him in his new pushchair, and take a walk to Central Avenue and 'bump into' Carole, Bianca or Angelica, who are guaranteed to be haunting the Cafe Nero on the corner. They'll swoon and gasp at the sudden arrival, but that will be okay, because Cassandra has spent those few months padding out her belly, just a little, and avoiding drinking wine with them, and suddenly cancelling plans, claiming that she feels 'a little off'. All things that will support her story that her pregnancy was 'touch and go', and she didn't want to jinx things in case they 'went south'. Her friends will be wonderfully put out, but they will feign understanding and tell her how brave she is to have done it alone.

And to have had her baby and lost her husband to a mugging gone wrong. Or perhaps him seeing his whore, which is what she guessed he was effectively doing, and lost in a tragic fire.

Michael, struggling though he was, had kept up his life insurance payments at her request, and that had panned out wonderfully.

Who cares about this land deal that is supposed to happen tonight? Fuck it. She didn't need it. Michael's untimely demise will keep her going quite happily. Perhaps she will invest in her own business. She had spoken to Ian about it in loose terms, opening a boutique or something in West Bridgford.

She is free now. Beholden to no man. Well, except the little one in her arms, and he didn't count. He belongs to her, not the other way round.

As Cassandra approaches the rise that leads up to the Marks and Spencer roof, she hears a scuffling behind her. Travis is stumbling unsteadily across the sloped roof and falling on to the flat one behind her. He looks up at her; he is scared, but determined.

He is a fool to follow her up here. She knows she is stupid for climbing across rooftops at any time, not just at night, in torrential rain, but what is he doing?

Cassandra shoots him a look, then lifts the baby up on

to the ledge, securing him as best she can, before leaping and heaving herself over too. She has always kept herself fit, working her core and upper body so that the physical effort required for her to do this is negligible.

She picks up the baby, and dashes across the large concrete expanse.

*

Travis almost slips off the tiled roof, painfully aware that if his body weight had been only a fraction to the right, he would have plummeted the twenty plus feet, head first.

He reaches out and lunges for the flat roof, leaping for all he is worth. Crashing into the gravelled surface, he feels the existing tear in his hip pull and twist, making him cry out in agony.

Blood saturates his jeans, mixing with the rainwater. He feels sick, his head feels light. Maybe it's the blood loss, maybe it's the heights.

Travis pushes himself up and sees Cassandra leaping effortlessly up the five foot ledge to the next roof. She scoops his son up and vanishes.

He runs as fast as he can, slamming into the wall. His fingers grip the edge and he jumps, the toes of his trainers hammering repeatedly onto the concrete, trying to find friction. His arms and shoulder burn with effort, his hip tears further, but after a minute of struggling, he rolls over onto the roof.

Gasping for air, he looks around. He realises he is on top of Marks and Spencer. The immediate area is large and flat, with little boxes, air-conditioning vents, protruding. Ahead, further levels rise up, like a grotesque game of Sonic or Mario, until the left quarter, where it looks like they drop down again.

Cassandra is running headlong for that. In fact, to his horror, she doesn't break stride, barely slowing before dropping away out of sight.

Travis is up and away again, but lacking Cassandra's obvious fearlessness, he slows long before he get the edge. Looking down, he sees it is only a few feet beneath, and Cassandra is already at the far edge.

From his vantage point, Travis can see a street beyond it, well below. A narrow, pedestrianised road that leads away to a T-junction, another one running left to right.

Cassandra is scuttling along the edge, peering down, seemingly searching for a way down, and apparently not finding one.

Emboldened by her evident lack of escape, he carefully eases himself onto the lower roof, and advances towards her.

He takes a breath, trying to make his voice sound big, 'Please, just give me my son. There's no way down from here.'

Cassandra wheels on him, her face contorted with venom, 'And just what the fuck do you think you're going to do, you little pussy?'

Travis tries to keep his expression the same, but she is right. What is he supposed to do? Fight her? Rip his son from her arms? There is the greatest chance they all fall off.

He banishes those thoughts. It is he who is in the right. She is wrong. She is the thief. 'It doesn't have to be like this. You can't take my son. It's not right!'

Cassandra scoffs, 'Take him? I bought him. He's mine.'

Travis now cries out, despite himself, 'You can't buy a baby! That's not right! It's not... you can't do it!'

'Supply and demand,' Cassandra hisses, 'You fucking moron. Camilla wanted rid of it, I wanted it. She needed money and I had money to give! It's the way the world works you naïve little prick!'

Anger boiling within him, Travis takes several steps forward, and to his surprise, Cassandra does take a few backwards, away from him.

Her eyes dart around, and her tone suddenly changes,

'Alright, things are pretty heated, okay? Let's look at things more logically.'

'No, give me my son! Now!' Travis feels braver, she is trying to negotiate. She is afraid. He can win this.

'Please, listen to me,' Cassandra continues, her voice adopting its husky, gentler tone, 'Assuming I gave him to you, where would you go? Where do you have to live? What would you feed him? How would you clothe him, school him, keep him safe?'

Travis has no answer. He has not thought of any of these things. He has been consumed with the idea of getting his son, not what they will do after.

Shit. What will they do? He has no money, no home. He literally had only the clothes on his back.

He didn't even have his guitar any more.

His expression is now at the mercy of his thoughts. Cassandra continues 'I have a house in a good area. It has good schools. I have a car. I have an income. I have time to devote to caring for him. He will never want for anything with me. I can give him everything he would ever need in life. I can give him a life.'

Cassandra takes a step towards him, softens her gaze and says softly, 'What can you give him?'

Travis stares back at her. His mind is racing. She is a liar; he can feel this about her, but everything she has said is truth. All he has is debt, an unpayable debt that will undoubtedly cost him his life.

Baxter is here. There is no escape for him. Even if Cassandra gives him his son, what can he do? Where can he go? Even on his own, he can't escape them, not for long. He knows what they will do to him.

Then what will become of my son?

Travis looks at her. She knows she is winning, so she makes one last play to bring it home.

She smiles, 'Let me pay you, Travis. Let me raise your son well, and let me help you along too. I have ten thousand pounds. Let *us* go home, and it's yours.'

Travis gulps. Every fibre in him says no. It's wrong. It's disgusting. It's cowardly.

And yet, with the rain lashing down on him, shivering with the cold and blood loss, he nods and holds out his hand.

22

As soon as the words are out of her mouth, Cassandra knows that she has made a mistake.

She does not have the £10, 000.

Camilla does. She took the envelope when she went to get the baby and did not come back with it. Either Camilla has hotfooted it to her new life with the money, or it is burning to ash in the flat.

That is all the cash she has in the world. Sure, she has assets and money tied up in the house, her car and other things, and a mountain of credit cards to see her through, but none of that can help her get Travis off her back right now.

His hand is held out to her, waiting for it, but his eyes

are averted. He is disgusted at himself.

Could she put him off? Say she needs to draw it out from a cash point? He doesn't appear overly bright; perhaps he would buy that. But then what? Try to run again, in the middle of town? First thing he will do is call the police, and then the whole God-damned thing will be blown.

Cassandra's thoughts get no further, as behind Travis, two heads appear over the edge of the rooftop. They are large men; one has a beard and some facial disfigurement. He shakes his head as he speaks.

'What the fuck are you two clowns doing up here?'

Travis takes a step away from him, shaking his head violently.

Cut Lip holds a finger out to him, 'Don't you move, bro. Seriously, nearly fucking killed myself getting up here.'

Cassandra watches as Travis takes another step away, towards her.

What is going on? Clearly he is terrified of them.

In a swift, practised movement, Cut Lip whips his handgun from his belt and points it at Travis, who almost seems to faint at the sight of it.

'I said don't move!' Cut Lip booms, then allows his eyes to cross to Cassandra. He studies her for a moment, takes note of the baby in her arms, and allows his eyes to travel slowly up and down her. He looks as if he's trying to work out who she is.

Cassandra understands this look, the glimmer of power it gives her, 'I'm not with him - '

'Shut it,' Cut Lip snaps, 'I don't really care what game you two cunts are playing; we can discuss it on the ground. So if you don't fucking mind?'

He uses the gun to motion that they should move past him, back up the rooftops, back to where they climbed up.

*

The flat is fully ablaze by the time they are back at the fire escape, flames and smoke billowing out of the open doorway there. It prohibits their descent there, so Cut Lip and his cohort find an alternative way down, further along, that drops down dangerously down at the front of the building, across the Marks and Spencer sign. Fortunately for them, people are looking at the fire itself, burning beyond St. Peter's Church, and do not notice four people and a baby climbing down from the roof of a department store.

Once on the ground, Travis feels as though he can barely walk, such is the dead weight in his stomach. Cut

Lip keeps the gun concealed now as he steers them through the crowds, taking them away from A Bar Called Cafe, and up Wheeler Gate instead.

Travis glances up at Cassandra, fear on her face, hushing and soothing his son in her arms, clumsily trying to quieten him. She feels his gaze and looks back at him. Although at odds with each other, both are scared and know that they have less to fear from one another than from these men.

Ahead, parked on the curb between trees are two Land Rover Discovery 3s, one black, one dark green. Their hazard lights blink rhythmically, almost tuned to Travis's footsteps.

As they approach, one of the driver's doors opens and Baxter steps out. He pulls the hood down from his head and stares coldly at Travis as he is brought to halt by the cars.

Gulping, Travis glances to his right, through the partly open rear window. Eyes are staring back at him.

Matt.

Baxter exhales long and deep, then grunts, 'I gave you a life line, Travis. I gave you an extra strike that I don't give to many other people because I felt your pain about your son. I have had bitches like that in my life. I wanted you to do right by the situation, by your son. But I spend two hours driving up here and find you climbing rooftops, chasing your missus here - '

He jerks his head at Cassandra, who is about to correct his inaccurate assumption about her, but gets a sharp look from Baxter.

She closes her mouth. She can take a hint.

Baxter returns his hard gaze to Travis, 'You spend the week I gave you fucking about, not raising my 10k? What kind of feckless idiot are you? I seriously cannot get my head around it.'

Travis opens his mouth, 'Baxter, I - '

Baxter turns swiftly, and grips Travis's jaw in a vice-like grip between his slender fingers, 'I've heard all I'm going to from you. Get them in the cars.'

*

Travis is shoved into the first car, alongside Matt, who stares hatefully at him. Baxter slides back into the front seat.

Turning, Travis can see Cassandra and his son being put in the second car. She looks as if she is about to resist, but is clearly shown another gun to persuade her.

The engine starts, the hazards are switched off, and they pull back out onto the road.

A Kiss At Midnight

Travis watches as they turn left onto Friar Lane, driving slowly as they pass revellers, drunk and cheerful, stumbling up and down the pubs and bars. No other care to them except where their next drink is coming from, and how much a taxi will charge them to get home. The wail of sirens cuts through the silence of the car; flashing blue lights fill the interior.

A pair of fire engines, their sirens booming fiercely as they approach the traffic lights, turn down Friar Lane, past them, heading towards St. Peter's Gate.

The car turns left down Maid Marion Way. As they pick up speed down the dual carriageway, sweep under the Arndale car park from where, only hours earlier, Travis had fallen, a glow can be seen reflected in the low cloud above the city.

A pulsing orange luminescence, thick black smoke rising up into the ubiquitous night sky.

To Travis, everything had begun there, and everything had ended there. That bar and the flat represent a glorious past with Camilla, and despite what she had done to him and his son, she will always be the love of his life. Where is she now? He had been so consumed with reclaiming his son, that he hadn't given her a single thought.

Had she got her money? Was she on a bus somewhere,

heading to plane?

A lump rises in his throat. Why couldn't she have involved him? Had faith in him, and let him prove to her that he would not only learn to be a good dad, but a great partner too?

Regret and despair, both constant life companions to him, sit on either shoulder as the rest of the journey passes too quickly.

Before Travis knows it, they are flying at speed across Clifton Bridge, and then sweeping under it in a circle, heading towards Wilford.

After a mini roundabout, they slow sharply and bump up a sudden left, though a barrier gate.

Travis realises that they are now right under Clifton Bridge, pulling up beside its enormous concrete supporting pillars. They skid to a stop on the loose stones, the second car pulling up beside them.

Silence for a moment as Baxter looks around, presumably ensuring the area is as quiet as it seems to be.

He nods, and gets out. Moments later, the rear doors open and both Travis and Matt are yanked out.

Travis is pushed towards the river, wide and pitch black, a faint gurgling as the water touches the rocky banks.

He turns around, and sees Matt, no longer allowed the comfort of his wheelchair, being dragged along behind him by two men.

Cut Lip follows last, his hand on Cassandra's shoulder, steering her towards him. Her icy resolve has now failed and her eyes are red with fearful tears.

A strong hand presses down on Travis's shoulder, encouraging him to drop to the ground. Matt is dropped alongside him, falling hard into the sharp stones. Cassandra is placed slightly more considerately with her tiny passenger.

He looks at his son. Cassandra has the back of her finger in his mouth, trying to soothe him. He sucks on it furiously, but whimpers every few moments.

Travis peers up at her. She is out of her depth. She doesn't know what to do with him any more than he would.

Keeping his voice low, Travis says to her, 'All they want is their ten grand. If you give it me, this is over. Please. I've agreed to you... raising my son... I just want us all to live.'

Matt, upon hearing this, raises his head. Genuine hope floods his eyes, and a part smile breaks across his face.

Cassandra doesn't look at them, but stares out at the river, writhing ever eastward in the darkness.

Travis frowns, glancing over his shoulder. The men now have the boots of the cars open, doing something there.

Baxter is talking to Cut Lip, pointing up and around, then back at them.

Travis hisses, 'Please. Please give them the money.'

Still nothing.

'Please!'

Cassandra's eyes flick to him, tears in them, 'I can't. I don't have it.'

'You said - '

'I know. Camilla has it... I... I'm sorry.'

Matt's head drops to the ground and he starts banging his head into the stones, his whimpering not unlike the baby's. Travis's mouth hangs open.

That's it.

There is nothing more to be done.

Then, as if in agreement, a sound, sharp and malicious, echoes across at them from the back of the car.

From Baxter's hand.

The scream of a drill.

EPILOGUE:
STRIKE THREE

Baxter and Cut Lip walk slowly back towards them; the former stoic, the drill hanging loosely from his hand, the latter grinning his gruesome, disfigured smile.

The rain clatters on the giant bridge above them, traffic at this hour having slowed to a trickle, still hissing loudly as it rumbles overhead. Water runs off the side, forming threads of liquid tumbling sixty feet and crashing into the stony ground.

One such cascade has formed a crash pool, smashing the stones aside and overwhelming the small crater. Water funnels out of one side, winding away downhill; a miniature river that eats its way past Travis.

He looks down at it fixedly. If he looks hard,

concentrates, it is not a tiny trail of rain water, it is a wide river, cutting its way through rocky banks and tumbling down cliff faces in some far off mountainous place, like Wyoming or Utah. *Is Utah rocky? Or is it more desert? Like, a rocky desert. What do they call that? Mesa?*

Footsteps. Coming closer. Crunching the stones. Echoing. The sound bouncing off the thick, grey columns and the solid ceiling high above.

Travis closes his eyes. He tries to picture Utah, or Wyoming or wherever except here.

Anywhere but here.

The crunching stops, and he knows that Baxter is stood before the three of them.

Forcing his eyes open, he sees Baxter's boots a few inches away, stood before him.

Oh God...

Nausea, sudden and violent, sweeps over him.

His eyes drift against his will, past Baxter's knee to his hand, to the drill hanging there.

A finger squeezes the trigger. The drill screams savagely, fast, then slow, on then off, like the revving of a sports engine.

Then, as if drawn by some force, Travis's eyes move upwards to Baxter's face. He is looking at him, his mouth pinched, eyes hard and without emotion.

Travis shivers. It is unclear whether it is from the cold and rain, or from fear.

Baxter sneers, snorts and glances at Cassandra, then jerks his head at Cut Lip.

Without a second's pause, Cut Lip steps forward and reaches down to Cassandra. She jumps, but seems relieved when, instead of grabbing her, he grabs the baby. Travis immediately cries out, moving towards Cassandra, lunging out to stop Cut Lip. A gun muzzle is pressed into Travis's head. He hesitates, and keeps shouting, 'No! No, please!'

Cassandra, taking a fraction too long to react, starts grabbing back at the baby as Cut Lip lifts him up from her.

'No! My baby!' she calls shrilly, 'Please, don't take my baby!'

She too is halted, by strong arms and another gun muzzle, as Cut Lip manoeuvres the tiny human into his arms and steps backwards.

Again in line with Baxter, he coos at the baby; a grotesque act, bunching his lips and making nonsense sounds.

Baxter steps towards them, moving the baby's collar so that he can see his face. The baby whimpers, half crying.

After a moment of study, Baxter looks at Cassandra and

Travis and nods, 'It's a good looking kid. You did well, both of you.'

Travis says nothing to correct him. Clearly, Cassandra now knows that confusing the issue with the truth of her relationship with both the baby and Travis, would not work in her favour.

Baxter narrows his eyes at the silence, thinking, and then he exhales. Without warning, he raises the drill above the baby's head, points the bit at its face and squeezes the trigger.

It is not clear which is louder, the dreadful scream of the drill, or the terrified cries from Cassandra and particularly, Travis.

The baby lets out a deafening wail at the sudden, obnoxious cacophony.

Travis, feeling that he is about to vomit, tries to rise but is stopped by strong hands. He struggles and has the blunt edge of the handgun smashed into his cheekbone.

The scream of the drill dissipates as Baxter releases the trigger, the echoing clatter of the rain returning.

Breathing hard, Baxter shakes his head at them and says, 'You think I'm a monster, Travis? I love kids. I have kids. I don't kill them, for fuck's sake.'

Baxter studies both Travis and Cassandra with disappointment, and then nods to Cut Lip, who passes the baby over to another man.

'But,' Baxter continues, 'You are not children. Any of you. And because of that, you must face the consequences of your actions. Be held accountable for the decisions that *you* have made. No more passing the buck. No more blaming each other, or the world, or the hand that you've been dealt.

'The position that you now find yourselves in, is of your own making.'

And with that, Baxter sucks his bottom lip thoughtfully, and says suddenly, 'I think we'll start with Matt.'

The two men standing by Matt suddenly grab him and pin him down, pushing his face into the ground. His eyes widen so much that for a second, Travis is reminded of Michael in his final moments.

Matt cries out, but it is not a scream, it is a sob, wailing and incomprehensible. Sounds, unidentifiable as words, only as verbal projectiles of raw, unfiltered emotion.

Pure, unrelenting terror.

Baxter crosses to him and crouches down, placing one of his knees on Matt's head, forcing the side of his face into the jagged stones.

Matt's rapid pleading is cut short, as Cut Lip forces a rag into his mouth, clamping it shut with his hand.

Cassandra, face contorted into a fear-twisted ugliness

she has never suffered, looks on, making little gasping noises. A hand falls on her, ready to cover her mouth if she screams.

Travis locks eyes with Matt. Fear, a fleck of anger, and mountains of seething blame aimed directly at him.

Baxter's finger on the trigger.

The drill awakens, screams for death, and descends.

The scream halts suddenly.

It is another trick, like with his son.

Baxter is not a monster.

He -

No. The pitch of drill is simply lower when the drill bites the skull. It tears through the thin skin of the scalp easily; it is the thick bone of the skull which presents the problem.

Minor capillaries are split, followed by more major veins and arteries. Dark red blood glugs out of the small hole, pulled up by the spiral indents of the bit; engineering doing its job. A sheet of the red fluid spills down Matt's face across his bulging eyes, as he bucks and writhes.

Baxter's arm tenses as he increases the pressure. It is not easy; the skull is dense, designed to protect the soft, important organ within.

Spittle works its way between the rag and the corners of

A Kiss At Midnight

Matt's mouth and Cut Lips fingers. Matt's scream is now long, inhuman behind its muffling.

Travis cannot look away. It is like he has discovered a gift. Cruel, much desired by man, to be coveted and feared. He is seeing his own future, albeit only minutes into it, and at once inescapable. Inexorable.

There is a pop, and the anger and blame vanish from Matt's eyes. There is a sudden peace there. No malice towards Travis, to pain, or fear or regret. The eyes soften, stop bulging out and they blink, sliding around in their sockets.

Baxter's hand drops a few inches in an instant, and he pushes down, rocking his wrist and turning the drill back and forth.

The light in Matt's eyes, peaceful and unafraid, goes out and it is over.

The drill ceases its terrible, piercing roar.

Breathing hard with exertion, Baxter stands up. He puts his free hand on Matt's head, and deftly uses a thumb to flick the drill into reverse. Gently squeezing the trigger, he backs the drill out into the air.

Redness drips from its end. Baxter flicks it a little. There is no stringy sinew this time, just blood, and little grey blobs, like discoloured jelly.

Baxter looks at his watch, then around to make sure

they are still not likely to be disturbed. He then lets his gaze fall on Cassandra and Travis.

*

It is as if her heart is going to explode.

Even in this situation, Cassandra wonders whether, if she presses her thumb up against the sensor on her smartphone and accesses the Fitness App, her heart rate will exceed 200? Surely it will; it is beating so fast her chest actually hurts.

She has seen dead bodies before. Two in fact; her mother's when she was seventeen, lying in the casket in the funeral home, looking pale and deflated; and her friend Christine's, who had over-dosed and died on a bathroom floor at a party.

But she has never seen anyone be killed. And definitely not like that.

Her first thought is, *I'm never going to be able to drive that image, the sight, the sound, and smell, not for years, if ever.*

The second thought is that there will be no years. She has only minutes left to live. She will not have to live with the memory of that awful sight; that thought alone offsets the fear that is eating away at her stomach.

A Kiss At Midnight

When Baxter looks at them both, with the blood of that poor man still dripping from the drill, she genuinely worries that she might defecate. She wonders if that man had, if Travis had, or would. That pathetic little creature; of course he would.

Sniffing, the cold, wet air obviously affecting his breathing, Baxter steps towards her, looking at her face, then down her body, then back up.

He stops, standing behind them both.

Cassandra glances over at Travis. His mouth is hanging open, the sort of mouth you make when you're trying to resist vomiting.

They don't know each other, and yet they are sharing something most people never will. It is a strange sort of intimacy, perverse and unwelcome, but oddly soothing. To be going to that place with someone.

Not alone.

When Baxter's hand falls on her shoulder, she feels all the breath in her body pour out of her mouth.

'I'm sorry,' Baxter says calmly, sincerity in his voice, 'that Travis dragged you into this.'

She closes her eyes tight, clamping her mouth shut.

Oh God, oh God, oh God...please don't let it hurt too much...

A bright light blasts through her eyelids. A divine light

that burns away all her past sins, absolves her, and welcomes her into the eternal after. Cries of the angels, the crushing of their wheels on the stones...

Cassandra snaps her eyes open. Baxter's hand is still on her shoulder, but like her, he is looking out towards the roadside where four cars are speeding towards them.

Two BMW saloons, a tall, stocky Audi, and a low-slung Jaguar. The men around her respond immediately, raising their guns, if they have them, as the cars skid to a stop.

Cassandra looks at Travis, who has now opened his eyes, and is looking at the newcomers.

The door of the Jaguar opens, but no one gets out.

Silence.

A nervous energy crackles under the bridge.

Eventually, a male voice, high and sing-song, but with an authority that can only come from nature asks, 'Who is that?'

Baxter frowns, squinting. His men shuffle nervously, fingers lightly brushing their triggers.

Baxter replies loudly, 'You need to tell me who the fuck that is!'

Another moment of silence, then, 'This is Fin Winston.'

It takes a second, but Cassandra looks up just in time to see Baxter's usually stoic face break into immediate defeat.

'Shit,' he mutters under his breath.

The voice comes back over, 'And who, might I ask, am I addressing?'

Baxter takes a breath and calls back, as confidently as he can, 'Baxter.'

'What?'

Baxter coughs, clearing his throat, 'Charlie Baxter. From the East End.'

'Do I know you?' booms the voice from the car's open door.

'No.'

'Do you know me?'

A beat.

'Yes.'

'Then why, might I ask, are the guns of your men still pointing at me?'

Baxter bites his lip hard, 'Fuck. Fuck! Get them down, you cunts. Now!'

He starts flapping his arms about, and no sooner have his men lowered their weapons, than the doors of the Audi and the two BMWs are flung open.

A dozen men, armed, but not pointing their weapons, step out, filling the wide space under the drenched bridge.

Breathing hard through his nose, Baxter waits, as the man finally gets out of the Jaguar.

Cassandra, her heartbeat slowly dropping, watches, allowing a shard of hope to penetrate her chest.

The man is very average-looking. Average build, height, looks. He wears a dark suit and rain coat, along with thin-rimmed, sports-style spectacles.

He descries the scene about him dispassionately; the mess that was Matt clearly does not bother him, but when he sees Cassandra, he smiles.

The man calling himself Finn says to Baxter, 'I do beg your pardon my intruding on your work here. My business is not actually with you, so you may relax, Mr. Baxter. It is with Mrs. Clavell that I wish to speak.'

Cassandra's throat tightens. Is this good or bad? This man is clearly not a good guy, if there were such a thing; but Baxter is most certainly the frying pan, is this Finn the fire?

Finn continues, 'May I approach?'

Baxter nods quickly, raising an arm in invitation. Finn starts to walk over, making a signal back towards the Jaguar. The rear passenger door opens and two men get out, one guiding the other. The latter is short, round and injured.

Ian!

Hope fills her as Baxter steps back and makes her stand. Her legs are wobbly with fear, and pins and needles, but she manages it.

Finn comes to a stop before her and Baxter, while Ian, clutching his right arm, halts with his escort right behind him.

Ian looks awful; bruised and exhausted. His eyes meet Cassandra's; she wants to ask him how he is, but daren't open her mouth.

Instead, her eyes go to Finn, who looks at the lump of meat that was Matt, then at the drill in Baxter's hand. Finn chuckles, 'Ah, Baxter, yes; I do know you by reputation. I'm pleased to see it is not a fiction, an urban myth. Brutal, but effective in ensuring debts are paid?'

Baxter grunts, jerks his head at Travis, 'Usually.'

Finn smiles, 'I see,' then turns to Cassandra, 'Well, it is actually your husband that I'm looking for. Do you, by chance, know of his location?'

Cassandra replies, but her voice is husky, her throat dry with fear, 'He's dead.'

Finn frowns, 'I'm sorry? Dead?'

This makes Ian look up in surprise, and Cassandra swallows, trying to lubricate her vocal chords, 'Yes. He died this evening. It was. - '

'That's not important,' Finn cuts her off, 'In fact, it

changes nothing. Fortunately, I have Mr. Clavell's accountant here, bruised though he is, to ensure that there is no break in the formalities.

'You were aware, Cassandra, if I may call you that, of your husband's planned sale of this property?'

Ian's escort passes Finn a file, and he holds it up to show Cassandra. It is the farmhouse and land. She looks at it and nods.

'Good, but you may not know that he gave me the right old run around this evening, refusing to agree to the offer of purchase. Our mutual friend Ian here has explained Mr. Clavell's frame of mind and I am, quite frankly, disgusted. It is just as well that he is no longer with us. I detest doing business with glorified car-salesmen-types like him. I hope you, as his next of kin, will be far more reasonable and, dare I say, mature?'

Cassandra glances at Ian, who tries to give her a look that encourages a yes. His arm looks sore, and his facial bruises appear very fresh.

Allowing a moment to think, she forces her mind to slow and gives this Finn her most amiable smile, 'You still wish to complete the sale? For me to sell you the property in my husband's place?'

Finn's smile is even more amiable than hers, and laced with an equal amount of insincerity, 'My dear Cassandra, you, like your husband, never had a choice in the matter. I have a substantial amount of money I need to sink into somewhere, and I have decided that your stinking, unsaleable farmhouse lot is the place to do it.'

Cassandra's keep her face polite, but suddenly her mind is screaming get out! This man needs to buy her property so that he can launder his money. It doesn't matter that it's a shit tip that's falling down, he just needs to filter money through it.

Finn is smiling at her. She knows that he knows that she has just worked it out. Cassandra is smart; it's how she has come so far in life from where she was.

'Of course,' Finn says, 'You will reap some of the benefit. The money does need spending.'

Cassandra knows this is dangerous, and these are dangerous people to be involved with, but these are the sort she has known for years. Whichever side of the law they claim to be on, a suit is a suit; they're all the same inside.

She offers her arm and says, 'It is a pleasure to be doing business with you, Mr. Winston.'

Finn allows her to thread hers through his and replies, 'You will certainly learn that it is.'

Cassandra allows a practised giggle, then stops suddenly, 'Oh, I'm sorry. My baby, may I - '

Finn's cordial smile vanishes, 'Let's not push our luck. Ian has already informed me of this ill-conceived plan to buy a baby. In this country? Surely you cannot be that stupid?'

Cassandra, feels her dream crumbling into dust. A man is telling her that she cannot have something.

Finn, seeing her reaction, says, 'Give it year. Let's get to know one another, get our new venture together really chugging along, then we'll see about getting you one from abroad. I here Chinese ones are all the rage right now. Oh, speaking of which - '

Stopping suddenly, Finn turns away from Cassandra and to Baxter says, 'I apologize to you, once again, Mr. Baxter, for interrupting your work. This baby, it belongs to this young man?'

He nods pointedly at Travis, who stares at them both silently. Baxter nods, 'Yeah. It's his.'

'Had a rough night, from what it appears?' and then to Travis, loudly, brashly, 'Had a bit of a crappy one, have you?'

Peering up through sopping ginger hair, Travis does not know how to reply. Finn laughs, 'What is his debt?'

'Ten grand.'

Finn snorts, 'Is that all? Well, as further apology to you, Mr. Baxter, and as thanks for your patience and respect, and in sympathy to a father who almost lost a son - '

Finn clicks his fingers at Ian's escort, who takes a wedge of pound notes wrapped in a band from an inner pocket.

Finn accepts it, counts several large notes out, only a fraction of the total, and hands them over to Baxter. He takes it, surprise evident on his face, but pockets it nonetheless.

Finn smiles, 'Good night to you, Mr. Baxter, and to you, young man. Come along, Cassandra, Ian. Let's find a nice late night bar, have a drink and sign some papers.'

Cassandra, having watched this exchange, is then led away. Towards the Jaguar. She looks back at Travis, still sitting silently on the ground.

She is seated in the lavish back seat, leather squeaking softly beneath her dress. Ian slides in beside her, and asks if she is okay, but she does not reply.

The engine purrs into life. The car pulls away, crunching over the gravel.

Ian is talking to her, Finn too, but Cassandra twists in her seat to stare out of the back window.

Cut Lip is now passing the baby back to Travis, still on the ground. He takes him timidly, unsure, but holds him to his chest.

The men, Cut Lip and Baxter, return to their own cars. The Jaguar turns a corner, bumping up onto the main road, and Travis and his son are lost from sight.

Tightness in her chest.

In her future is more money than she can spend; she can fill her driveway with car and her home with furniture, but, she fears, her arms will always be empty.

*

Travis sits on the cold, wet stones. His clothes are soaked through. His hand, aching from the drill a week before, his side, slashed by Cassandra's knife, stings, though it has stopped bleeding. He is shivering so hard his teeth hurt. The only warmth comes from the tiny body cradled in his arms, and that is rapidly fading.

Travis opens his damp coat, tucking his son inside. It helps a little, helps them both. Little hands reach up and Travis takes one. A fist wraps around his finger, eyes looking up at him for a moment, and it looks like a smile appears on his son's face.

It goes again, replaced by a little cry, a prelude to more.

He is hungry. They both are.

Travis looks at him, but there is something missing.

A name. He has no name. How can someone have no name? It is the very fabric of a person's existence.

Or is it?

His son has existed quite happily for weeks without one; maybe a name is not that important a thing. *Perhaps it does not define you. It is a just a sound we cry, and we, in our wise folly, attach the meaning.*

Nothing more.

Nonetheless, Travis thinks, he *will* need one.

But later. Food first.

He stands, shakily and looks out across the wide, dark river, the pouring rain and the traffic thundering overhead, and has a thought. With what, exactly will he buy this food?

Objective complete. He has what he claimed he desired more than anything, but literally nothing else.

His old friend despair sidles up to him again.

Cassandra was right, what can he offer his son?

Not even a single meal on a wet night.

His hands shake, with cold and fury at the universe; he is not evil, he does not deserve this, surely. His baby son certainly does not.

A new thought drifts into his mind, as if swept in on the soaking wind.

Perhaps I do deserve all this.

His entire life has been dedicated to finding a quick and easy path to success, to money, to happiness. He has not wanted to work for it, not too hard, at least; he has tried everything from scratch-cards to cash-in-hand jobs to the ill-thought out burger van venture.

The result of these is nothing more than misery, heartbreak and death. He has lost his friend, lost the love of his life, and almost lost his son.

And it didn't have to be that way.

He made it that way.

It is his fault.

He deserves it all.

Travis, pity biting at him, grimaces. He shoves his cold, free hand into his pocket and stops.

There is something there. Something he had forgotten about.

And it is nothing, and it is everything. It will not go far, if used badly, but it will start them off. A meal, then maybe shelter, clothes, then maybe nothing.

But it is hope.

It is redemption.

Provided by a rotund accountant who didn't understand its value beyond the fiscal.

Four hundred and sixty five pounds of it.

A Kiss At Midnight

A Kiss At Midnight

Acknowledgements

Thanks to everybody who has helped with this book, either with the many unnecessary spelling and grammatical mistakes that I make, or by giving the first draft a read and being honest about it, or simply by listening as I ramble on about it.

Thanks to my wife, Lynsey, whose ongoing support is genuinely invaluable, as is her ability to keep me where I should be, when I should be there, as I seem to constantly live in fantasy land. I can depend on her for the most honest and brutal criticism.

Grace M. Cooper, my fellow writer (*Guilt*, check it out!), whose own talent keeps me striving to get better, is always happy to give my initial, messy and incomplete drafts a read, and provide honest and comprehensive feedback. Fantastic online book reviewer Jade Grass who is always first in line to read, review and share my new work and is, I feel, very kind.

Finally, the biggest thanks to Daemian Greaves, who to be honest, had the most difficult job in editing the mess that was my first draft, putting in an incredible amount of work to make it coherent and legible, and as a result, enjoyable! His advice on grammar, sentence structure, word use and all the rest of it is vital, although at times can make me feel rather dumb, but I wouldn't change it.

A Kiss At Midnight

A Kiss At Midnight

Read the first chapter from the
chilling short thriller

EPITHALAMIUM

also by Nick Archer

1

Julian can hear their cries as clearly now in his mind as when he first heard them. Shrill voices, fractured by the crushing weight of fear.
Terrified.
Begging.
He licks his dry lips, regretting it immediately. They sting. An icy gust blows at them, making them sting with pain. Instinctively he runs his tongue over them again, trying to protect them against the biting chill and only making it worse. Perpetuating his suffering.
'I said are you okay?'
The voice is harsh and annoyed. Each word is over-pronounced like the speaker is talking to an idiot.
Julian's eyes refocus. The cries in his mind retreat to the

back of it, albeit only for a small time, he knows. Through the drifting flakes, an obnoxious white glare of LED headlights appears, set at too high an angle. Another gust sends the flakes into a swirling dance. Movement beyond them, a sigh.

A face is staring at him, skin cracked with age, eyes narrowed, a tall, liver-spotted brow furrowed in irritation. A pair of hands jerk, palms open, inviting a response.

'David, get back in the car.' Another voice. This one from inside the car, female, and Julian's eyes snap to her, 'He's clearly not with it. Leave him and let's get home before the roads seize up.'

David doesn't move, his gaze locked on Julian. He speaks again, louder, but this time with genuine concern, 'Do you need help?'

Julian's heart begins to pound, and he squints through the fluttering white particles and the misty glare of the headlamps. A woman sits in the passenger's seat, her own gaze shifting from Julian to David and back again. Light hair and blue eyes, this much only he can discern in the gloom. Julian cranes his neck and raises his hand to block out the dazzling white.

'What are you looking at?' David's tone has now lost its empathy, replaced with a territorial terseness. Julian knows it well. He'd used it many times. Right now, however, all his attention is focused on the woman in the car staring back at him.

Julian steps forward, trying to find a position where the painful light projected at him is diminished. Orange light pulses at the side of his face, from the corners of his own car beside him.

Blue eyes. Light hair. Good.

Excitement and fear collide in the pit of his stomach.

The weight in the back of his waistband increases tenfold and his legs feel suddenly weaker.

With his left hand, he manages to block some more light.

A narrow chin. High cheekbones. Promising.

Julian's right-hand moves around his back to his sagging leather belt and his fingers wrap around the pistol's grip, pulling slightly, easing the burden.

David watches him, and Julian can somehow feel the tension rise, even across the several yards that separate them on the quiet road.

The isolation of that stretch of broken tarmac has suddenly become all too apparent. A half mile from junction to junction, one ahead and one behind. Parallel to them is a dual carriageway, the hissing of the passing heavy traffic squeezing between the dark factories and warehouses between it and them.

David's hand on the top of the door moves. Clearly, in his late seventies, it's obvious that he isn't a man who is easily scared but has endured into his golden years by having a keen instinct for danger, and a blend of intuition and experience hard won by those gathering winters. He is about to make a primal decision.

Fight or flight.

In her seat, the woman leans forward a little. The mist of oppressive light clears a little and Julian can finally make out her face.

Lines.

Dried up rivers and tributaries cut across an undulating expanse of time-weathered skin. Her papery complexion a shadow of former beauty, lost to all but those who knew her in her glorious youth.

Julian relaxes. The tension goes from his shoulders, the grip loosens on the grip of the heavy gun, the weight returns to his lower back. He lets his jacket cover it.

Relief and frustration are a cocktail of agony for him. He turns suddenly away from them, unable to look at them any longer.

The snow has slowed. Leaving the road still black and untouched. Only a few flakes fall amidst the rhythmical orange glow of the hazard lights of Julian's car.

He closes his eyes and rubs his hand across his balding scalp. Behind him, he can hear the woman hissing at David, and the scraping of his boots on the road's battered surface.

Julian sighs and speaks, 'I'm fine. Sorry to have bothered you.' And he turns to look at them over his shoulder, smiling as warmly and as apologetically as he can, 'Please apologise to your wife for me. I'm sorry if I scared her.'

The older man clears his throat, his voice tight. He is indeed tensed and ready. 'That's quite alright. Do you need help?'

Julian smiles again, and shakes his head. 'No, I'm okay. I'm just waiting.'

David waits a moment before he replies, the conversation, and the situation, at a crossroads. Then he nods and gets silently back into the car.

Julian steps out of the middle of the road, against his own car door and uses the roof to support himself.

The other car's engine revs, hot air blasting from the back, in a plume of exhaust. It pulls around and moves past Julian. David gives him a curt nod as they pass, the woman's eyes are wide and judgemental, and then they are both gone.

Julian has already gotten back into his car by the time they have turned the corner at the end, settling in to wait some more. In the silence, the tortured cries charge from the back of his mind to torture him once more.

A Kiss At Midnight

A Kiss At Midnight

Praise for
EPITHALAMIUM

Reviews from Amazon

'Grips you from the start and won't let go!'

'Fabulous story. Tip: reserve your afternoon because once you start you won't be able to put it down until you've finished it'

'Each chapter ends on such a cliff hanger that you are compelled to keep reading, I really enjoyed this and would definitely recommend it!'

'Very easy to read in one sitting, and not just because it is under 110 pages - this is a genuine page-turner. It grips from the start and continues at a relentless pace. Consistently tense, exciting, and unpredictable, this Nottingham-set thriller is an excellent read.'

'Much enjoyed! Kept me guessing. Nice little page turner.'

Review from Goodreads

'Wow, this was a gripping story! I read it in one sitting, as I could not stop. Epithalamium tells the story of Scarlett, a young woman who suddenly finds herself in mortal danger, taken from her home one evening. The tale twists and turns, and all is not as it

appears, as Scarlett's situation gradually worsens as the night goes on. Just when I though I knew what was going to happen, the story took another turn. The characters were believable, and the reader can feel the terror that Scarlett must have felt. If you are after a chilling novella, Epithalamium is a must-read. 4 Stars.'

A Kiss At Midnight

Nick Archer is writer and film-maker from Nottingham, UK. He has a profound passion for film and enjoys telling stories either on screen, or on the page.

OTHER WORKS BY

NICK ARCHER

Novels

Available on Amazon

A Kiss at Midnight

Haiku-Noir

A Kiss At Midnight

Short Films

Available on Amazon Prime

Broken

Car Park

Gemini

Honeytrap

Shoulder to the Plough

Arabesque

Stairwell

A Kiss At Midnight

A Kiss at Midnight
Nick Archer
© *Copyright, All Right Reserved 2018*

Printed in Great Britain
by Amazon